THE ROSE AND THE REBEL

In stifling summer heat, Miss Penelope Rose decides to take a swim — scandalously, in an outdoor pool on her father's estate. Having sent off her maid, Penelope strips to her underclothes and indulges herself in the coolness of the secluded water. But when she climbs out, wearing only her soaked chemise, her dress has disappeared! To make matters considerably more embarrassing, she finds herself standing face to face with the culprit — Mr Lucas Bleakly, the eligible bachelor son of the local reverend . . .

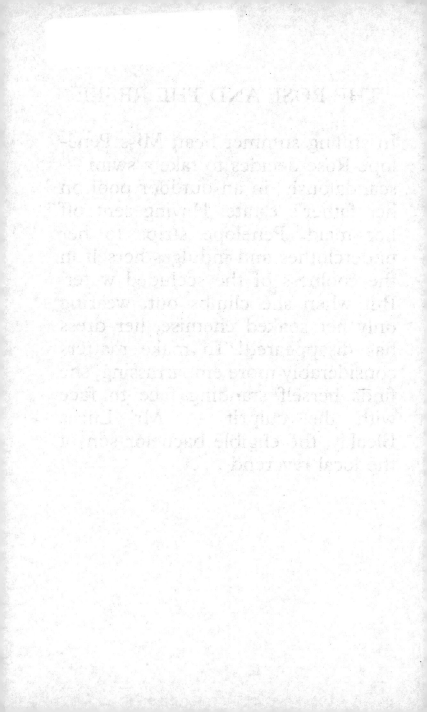

VALERIE HOLMES

THE ROSE AND THE REBEL

Complete and Unabridged

LINFORD
Leicester

First published in Great Britain in 2017

First Linford Edition
published 2017

A catalogue record for this book is available
from the British Library.

ISBN 978–1–4448–3399–7

1

Penelope enjoyed the woodland. She was safe here; they would both be safe so long as they stayed true to this well-used path. It was still on her father's land, although it used a shortcut from the old vicarage to the town. The occasional neighbour from the village might ride a horse or small wagon along its rutted surface, as it avoided the steeper bank from the moor road down to the vale, but others — strangers — were discouraged by a sign stating that the track was 'Private Land'.

Penelope happily walked along in the stifling heat as Cuthbertson, her maid, tried to keep up with her. It was unusually hot, even for the summer season, and the older woman looked flustered as her shorter legs tried to keep pace with Penelope's younger ones. The woman's heart was simply not in the adventure in any sense of the word.

'Do you need to rest?' Penelope asked.

She watched the bonneted head shake in defiance. 'No, miss, but perhaps you should . . . ' she added, with more than a hint of hope in her voice.

Penelope had eagerly left the Hall as she was finding her daily life very restricting. It felt like everyone around her was reminding her constantly, at every turn, that she was a young lady; and that heatwave or not, she was expected to dress and act appropriately. If she was to find a good husband, then she must both be chastened and look pale. Penelope closed her eyes for a moment as she waited again for Cuthbertson to catch up with her. She tilted her face up to the sun as it shone through the leaves of the tall trees. Her bonnet was meant to shield her face, but Penelope wanted to throw it up into the branches and be free to enjoy the unusual warmth in all its glory.

'Sorry, miss, my boots is rubbing,' Cuthbertson said, slightly breathlessly. 'You should not look at the sun. It will burn your eyes and turn your skin.'

Cuthbertson's dress was made of a heavier, more durable fabric, and Penelope felt a sudden tinge of guilt for the woman, as she had given no thought to her discomfort and lack of alternative apparel to change into at the end of their walk. She would have to stay in her sweated garment until night-time. Penelope raised an eyebrow at her; perhaps she would not care, she thought. The previous excuse Cuthbertson had given had been that her hair had slipped out of her hat and needed fixing.

Penelope was also feeling the heat; her walking dress was loose, as she had not worn her corset today. She suppressed a smile at the thought of the impropriety, as it was indeed bad of her not to be properly attired when she left her own bedchamber, let alone the Hall, but who was there to know? She had thought the woodland would be cooler and offer much-needed shelter, perhaps even a cooler breeze. It did, a little, but this place of her childhood held one secret place that she longed to enter, although not with Cuthbertson in tow. If her mother and father knew what was on her mind, she would be locked in a room until a suitor carried her away to safety.

Penelope had told her maid to stay behind — but, oh no, she had insisted on coming, as Penelope had to be accompanied everywhere; and so, in anger, Penelope had made Cuthbertson suffer. She could see beads of sweat on the woman's forehead and her cheeks seemed high in colour — not just with annoyance at her younger charge, but because she was struggling against the heat.

Her own stockings, petticoats and chemise were layers that Penelope would willingly cast off. It was humid, and she longed to slip into the cool pool she had swum in as a child — whenever her father was away, that was. Why couldn't she now? A smile played on her lips. Looking at her companion, she glanced down at the woman and decided she would try one last ploy. She would be generous and kind.

'Cuthbertson, please go back to the Hall and fetch my parasol. It is just too hot for me to walk any further without it.' Penelope's suggestion obviously took the older woman by surprise.

Cuthbertson looked at her with a mixture of pleasure and dread. It was a good half-hour walk back through the woodland path to the Hall. The thought of returning to the cool of the servants' quarters obviously appealed to her, but she did not seem so keen to have to return again to Penelope with a parasol.

'Miss, I shouldn't leave you here. Perhaps we should both return . . . ' She looked at her with hopeful puppy dog eyes. They did not move Penelope.

Penelope rounded on her. She felt

slightly cruel, for she knew Cuthbertson had not been in their service long, and needed the position as her husband had been killed in the war against Napoleon's army. The war may be over now, but the damage to the local community — all the men they had lost, the broken lives of the returning injured and the widowed — lingered.

'I am not used to being questioned!' she snapped. Then, in a more kindly manner, added, 'Father and Mother will be out for most of the day. So please return and fetch my parasol. However, you may help yourself to some of the fresh lemonade from Cook, and then once you are rested and refreshed return to me here. I will sit here a while on the tree trunk over there, and read my little book. I will be in the shade and will patiently await your return.'

With only a slight hesitation, Esther Cuthbertson said, 'If you are sure you will not stray and will keep well in the shade, miss?' She was looking around as if assessing the woodland for danger.

Penelope nodded and set to making herself comfortable on the tree stump before taking out her small book from her pocket. Hesitantly, her maid nodded and walked away.

Penelope watched until the woman had turned the corner, disappearing from view. She then ran on another hundred paces until she came to the hidden place of yesteryear. There, she slipped down the narrow pathway between two large boulders to the edge of a small waterfall, and into her childhood hiding place.

She paused momentarily, as the ground near the pool was moist from the spray, and removed her hat and boots. Not wanting to stain her stockings, she rolled them down and carefully wrapped the silk around itself until each one was a tight roll, and placed them inside her hat. Next, she unhooked the front of her walking dress, and inverted it so it too could be left on dry land hidden by the large stone outcrop. She felt the warmth of the sun on her bare arms, refreshed by the spray. Then her petticoat was removed over her head, and it too was rolled up inside-out. Once down only to her chemise Penelope felt totally liberated.

Finally she repinned her hair to make it tighter than it had been so that it would not come tumbling about her shoulders. Penelope smiled, and stifled a giggle as, childlike, she slipped into the pool with ease. It was cool. It was refreshing. The feeling was everything she remembered.

Knowing full well what she had intended to do, her corset had been left tucked under her bed covers. Penelope had stared at her body in the looking-glass enough times to know it was slender. Her firm breasts welcomed the chill of the fresh water covering her skin as she swam around in small circles. She dared not move far out from the side, for there was a stronger current nearer the falling water as it entered the calm of the pool. Penelope was a competent swimmer, but knew her strength was limited against the forces of nature, and further so by the lack of opportunity to swim regularly as she had before she became a woman.

Delighting in the freedom of movement and the sensation of being at one with nature, her senses were totally alive.

For the last week, the heat had been more stifling by the day. The temperature, her father had said, was befitting that of the colonies. He should know, for he had been as far as the lands of the East India Company.

Her mother had therefore insisted that she stay within the Hall, wearing her full attire, even though there was no one to see or know. She had standards to uphold and her dignity in front of the servants.

Penelope dismissed such thoughts and kept her head above the water. Her time there seemed short, reluctantly she stepped out. It was then that Penelope saw that her clothes had vanished.

2

Dripping and hardly decent in her sodden chemise, Penelope stared around the pathway between the boulders, only to see the unmistakable imprint of a man's boot in the wet mud. She stood stockstill, aware of the fabric clinging to her skin, and pulled it away from her body. Swallowing deeply, aware that she was no longer a child — as too would be anyone who looked upon her now — she felt a wave of panic well up inside her. How stupid she was! There was no point in running. Where could she go, looking as she did? If seen, she would be ruined and damned. Her folly was starker and had further-reaching consequences beyond merely the theft of her garments.

Children! It was a childish prank. If it was young Glen the gamekeeper's son, then she could bribe him; he was always sneaking in to see their scullery maid,

Agnes, against his father's wishes. She hoped beyond hope it was him for, humiliating as that would be, at least she could contain and control the situation. He was given to embellishing tales, so once she was safely back at the house, if he gossiped no one would believe him. He would no doubt be in a deal of trouble if he did. If it *was* him . . .

'Show yourself, you coward!' she ordered, her fists clenched at her side.

There was no sign of movement ahead of her, but above her head, atop one of the boulders, the tall figure of a man complete in riding outfit stood looking down on her. Never had Penelope felt so small and insignificant in all her eighteen years. Shame washed over her as if she was stark naked in front of him. She wanted to scream, run, flee or throw herself back into the cool waters, but no action she could take could make her situation right. She was trapped.

'I am no coward, miss. But you are

one brazen young minx. You either have no reputation to protect, no life worth any notable value, or you are bordering on insane.' His deep voice seemed to roll down the boulder and hit her hard, as each word he uttered was undeniably true.

'How dare you talk to me in that manner? Give me my clothes back now!' Penelope was trying not to shout at him. Her temper so near to the surface had made her forget that, in the warmth and heat of the day, she faced him almost naked. Decency had left her, and with it her senses. 'You are no more than a common thief!' she accused.

'What possessed you to do such a stupid thing? Do you realise you risked your life in there?' he asked and calmly sat down on the rock, his legs dangling over the edge above her.

'I know this place well, and what is more, I am a strong swimmer!' She was defiant but, as she glanced back at the pool, she could see how high the water level was, and further into the centre of the pond the water whirled in a way that she had not remembered it doing when she was a child. The cascade from the waterfall seemed to almost perpetuate the momentum of the underlying circling current.

'You may be a tolerably decent swimmer in calm shallow waters, but here it is strong in current; although how you came to be a swimmer at all bemuses me.' He pointed to the top of the small waterfall. 'If it should rain suddenly and heavily — as well it may, if the heat breaks — then this area would be hit by a torrent of water, and the pool that has already begun to swirl would grow in strength and speed. You, foolish young wench, would have to transform from wood nymph to mermaid, or drown.' He shrugged his shoulders. 'What a choice!'

'Mermaids live in the sea,' she said almost childishly, folding her arms across her breasts and hoping that her body was covered, even though there was little she could do about her calves, ankles or feet. 'My clothes, please,' she said in a calmer manner.

'Seeing as you ask me nicely, you may have them; but you, miss, will be in a great deal of trouble when news of this adventure reaches your father.'

Panic filled her, replacing and far overtaking her feelings of shame. Did he know who she was? 'No! Please. He must not know. He would not survive the shame of my behaviour and I'd be sent to . . . '

'A convent?' he said, staring down at her.

'Please, don't. I behaved badly, but . . . '

'You behaved like a simpleton or a daring trollop,' he said, staring at her bemused reddening face.

Her eyes watered. She was completely undone, as her mother would say when she gossiped about a young woman's lack of dignity. Her parents would never forgive her.

A broad smile slowly appeared on the

man's face, a face that began to show an impish quality as well as his previous strength of character. However, it also revealed that he was well aware that she could be ruined by just being with him alone — even fully dressed, let alone in her present dishevelled state. Penelope felt the blood rush around her veins and had to swallow to fight back the emotions that ran wild within her heart.

She had wanted to be a naughty child again, yet here she was, completely disgracing herself in front of a total stranger. A horrid notion crossed her mind. What if he was known to her father? His words might not be an idle threat.

He disappeared from her sight and she was filled with a growing sense of dread. Then she saw him at the top of the pathway, filling the gap between the boulders, standing only a few steps away from her. She swallowed, bracing herself as he stepped forward. What if he attacked her? What if he grabbed her? She would be unable to save herself. Anxiously, she glanced at the water. Surely she would have a better chance in there, even if she had to clamber to the far bank and run through the woods half-naked to try and slip back into the Hall at night. She was about to throw herself back into the water to escape him when he shouted to her. All humour had left his expression.

'No!' he said. 'Please, don't.' He placed her clothes back on the ground and then backed away with his hands held up by the sides of his shoulders. 'I have teased you long enough. I merely wanted to make you see the danger of your situation so that you would never be so reckless again. When you are dressed respectably, I will be waiting for you on the path just through there.' He gestured with his hands toward the track. 'I will walk you back to safety at the Hall.' He then turned and left her line of sight.

Penelope said nothing more in response, closing her eyes momentarily, for he knew her well enough. She was known to be from the Hall. Her shame was so great, and yet all she had wished to do was cool down and swim. She felt like Eve, having been caught out in the Garden of Eden, suddenly aware of her own nakedness and ashamed at her behaviour. However, Penelope's defiant nature still bridled against such notions. She had enjoyed the feel of the water as it caressed her body. Why should she not be able to enjoy nature in all its beauty when it was on their land? The answer was always the same: because she was a female. The stranger could have done the same as she, and everyone would have admired his physical strength and daring. Still, Penelope thought ironically that she had had her wish, as she was now cool and still quite damp.

She quickly rubbed herself as dry as she could with the inside of her walking dress. Penelope knew the back of the skirt would look crumpled, but she had to do something, and quickly. Once her legs were no more than slightly damp, she rolled up her stockings and pulled on her boots, then wrapped her nearly dry body and moist chemise into her walking dress. The hat was placed atop her hair; she was grateful that at least that had held in place. Satisfied that she was decent again, she stepped into the gap between the boulders, but was short of stepping out onto the track when she heard a horse whinny and a brake being applied to a vehicle. There was now not one male voice there, but two.

'Lucas! Whatever has delayed you? Your mother expected you back over an hour ago.'

The speaker was definitely familiar to Penelope. The name Lucas was not, but the owner of the voice definitely belonged to Reverend Willis Bleakly. If he found her here with a stranger in such a place, she had no doubt that her father would completely disown her!

'Father, I dallied to admire the beauty and cool of the small waterfall.

It is, after all, some time since I have seen it.' Her stranger was calm in his retort, but she was now ready to pray, as she wished and hoped beyond hope that he did not give her away. Why he should protect her, she could not imagine, but her father's anger would spill over into the county if he was told of her downfall by Bleakly, his long-time adversary.

The stranger was the son of the priest. Penelope held her breath. She felt as if she would never breathe easily again. Could her situation become any worse? Yes, of course it could, and very quickly. This man Lucas could destroy her, and in so doing he would cause the complete destruction of her father also. Penelope closed her eyes as she envisioned the effect such shame would have on her mother. Her father was outspoken against the church, Bleakly's affluent lifestyle as he preached of sin to his flock, and the offerings so disproportionate to the facilities for the poor of the parish. Bleakly had even called her father a rebel and threatened to have him arrested if he uttered such blasphemous words to him in another soul's hearing.

'Your mother is quite frantic. You should have more respect!' The reverend was very annoyed. 'Go and try to make amends. Or is it your wish to be one constant disappointment to her?'

'I apologise, Father, for being late, but I did tell her that I had no wish to meet the young lady she had invited to visit this afternoon.'

'You could at least be civil. You have returned to us, and your mother only wishes you to meet a suitable lady who can provide you with . . . '

'I will return directly. Were you on your way to town, sir?' Lucas Bleakly interrupted his father's words. Penelope had become engrossed in this conversation, as it appeared that the man had enough problems of his own and did not wish to add her dilemma to them.

'Yes, Lucas, I am, as I have duties to perform, unlike you. I respect and serve my parishioners. Dally no more! You will meet Miss Henderson and you will be personable to her. She is from a very good family. Her father is a military man who came from a long line of moneyed officers.'

Penelope did not dare to look, but heard the horse snuffle.

'You will be late, Father,' Lucas said.

'Be sure you go there with haste and make some acceptable and rational excuse for your earlier absence.'

Penelope heard the gig move on. She waited until the younger man's face appeared around the edge of the boulder and smiled at her.

'It is safe for you to appear now, my little wood nymph,' he said, not in the least embarrassed by the exchange with his father.

'Shouldn't you be going to your mama?' she asked. The hint of sarcasm in her voice made him smile even more broadly.

'Ah, the nymph has teeth when she is attired.' Her comment was returned in kind. He stepped back so that she could walk out onto the path.

'Your father seems vexed with you, Mr Lucas Bleakly.' She walked into the open, flicking her skirts so that the hem hung straight down.

'Indeed, he often is, I am afraid.'

'Are you a disobedient son?' she asked.

'Like you, Miss Penelope, I am a bit of a rebel in their eyes. Although, to be truthful, you would be beyond the pale should he know of your antics.' His smile faltered as if there was a rebuke thinly hidden within the words.

She glared at him and was about to answer his insult, despite it being true, and therefore founded, but she heard the out-of-breath shout from Cuthbertson approaching.

'Miss! Miss, you must come home! Miss . . . '

'Goodbye, nymph,' he said. He bowed slightly, touching the rim of his tall hat, and walked briskly away. Penelope did not look back at him;

instead, she took a deep breath, and strode at a pace to join her rather agitated maid.

3

'What is the meaning of summoning me back in such a fashion?' She passed Cuthbertson, leading her away from Mr Lucas Bleakly. 'And where is my parasol? Did you go all that way back to the Hall just to have your cooling drink, only to forget the purpose of your return?' Penelope snapped as she stormed along the path, with Cuthbertson almost running to keep up with her.

'Yes, I forgot it, but only when I heard that your mother had returned earlier than you expected. She was fetched back in the carriage, miss. I thought I should come and get you before you was missed. That's if I could get back here in time — ' Cuthbertson stopped mid-path and shouted the next words at her mistress. 'Of course, I had no idea you was having an assignation and did not wish to be disturbed!'

Penelope stopped and quickly turned, not without glancing around her to make sure that it was only trees that could have heard her maid's accusation. Cuthbertson was biting her bottom lip, either in vexation or in controlled anger, but the woman did not flinch or step back as Penelope stood before her. Instead of cowering, she merely stared back at her defiantly.

'How dare you speak to me in such a way!' Penelope's voice was lowered. She had no wish to attract anyone's attention if the woman was going to start shouting accusations at her.

'I dare to because I have been used as a fool, and though in need of this position, I am no one's fool.' The woman sighed as Penelope opened her mouth to retort, but Cuthbertson had not finished with her. 'I only mean, miss, that you chased me back off to the Hall purposefully, and then I find you with young Mr Lucas Bleakly from the parsonage. His reputation is known, miss. He nearly got thrown out from his Oxbridge schooling; he finished it, but then refused to join the faith and follow the family tradition, and now is here. Word has it that he has already been seen chatting to Miss Henderson from Beckton Hall over in Beckton Vale. And now, well, if you'd been seen meeting with him, here alone, in the woods . . . ' She glanced down at the damp hem of Penelope's dress. 'You've been near water, miss?'

'You will say nothing of this. Do you hear me?' Penelope snapped. 'You have said far too much already. I think you should remember . . . '

'What? That I was not born yesterday, as you were? Why should I remember anything — for isn't it you, miss, that should remember who you are? What you are? And in so doing, perhaps think on how everything what you do can reflect badly on your poor father? Or are you going to threaten me with dismissal for trying to cover your back? I was trying to make sure you got back in time to see your mother before she banned you from leaving the Hall without her permission until you are wed!' She tilted her head on the side and glanced at Penelope, slowly up and down. 'Your back, miss, is inexplicably wet,' she added.

'It was not what you think. He came across me. We had no 'assignation', as you put it. I don't even know the man. He was merely out for a walk. It was completely innocent. I merely wished to see the old pool and stay out of the sun whilst I awaited your return. How was I to know that Mr Lucas Bleakly had the same notion? I may be many things, but I am no mind reader!'

'Did you stumble across him accidently and happen to fall in the water? Because I can smell it on you. A sort of natural pond smell,' she added sarcastically, and sniffed the air.

'I don't like your tone.' Penelope was taken aback when the woman laughed at her.

'No, well, I've not been taken too

much by yours recently, either.'

'I am not threatening you with dismissal. I did a foolish thing staying in the woods on my own. I had no idea that man was anywhere near me, and neither did I know who he was, as I do not listen to idle tittle-tattle.'

'Then perhaps, miss, you should start to.' Cuthbertson raised an eyebrow, challenging Penelope further.

'So why has Mother returned so soon?' Penelope quickly changed the subject.

'She was taken over all faint apparently. It could just be the heat, her age and weight, miss, or she may have just wanted to return to the cool of the Hall whilst your father saw to his business. Whatever the reason, she is in her room at the moment, but will be asking for you as soon as she has her lemon water and her clothes are changed. So, what do I tell her you have been up to, miss?' Cuthbertson looked at her with wide-open eyes. They were far from innocent.

'You tell her nothing. I will talk to her

as soon as I slip into another dress. And please do not exchange idle tittle-tattle with the other servants in order to win their favour.' Penelope tried to copy her mother's style of high-handedness with the servants, but it just was not working on Cuthbertson. The woman was too worldly for Penelope to be able to stare down.

'Miss, your pa gave me this position. He told me he wanted me to be looking out for you, as you had ran circles around the unsuspecting young maid you had previously. I told him that I would do that for him, as I needed to keep this position. And I will, if you don't go sending me on any wild goose chases again, or I will report to him on your most recent antics. You could have been ruined by being seen with that man.'

'No one has seen us!' Penelope still bridled despite having no valid defence.

'Funny, I thought I saw the reverend disappearing down the road in his gig as I came over the brow of the field.'

'You did, but he did not see me. Mr Lucas chatted with his father, but I was not a part of the conversation.'

'Just as well, then! But, lass, you could have been ruined by that man and no one would have known but you and him. How would it go down with your father if his wild child had been raped — yes! I mean that word, and you know what I mean by it; you have read it in the Bible yourself, no doubt.'

'He is a priest's son!' Penelope said, hardly believing the woman could be so outspoken as to even suggest such a thing.

'Yes, a priest's son! Who would believe you had not acted wantonly and willingly? He is already seen as a cad, a man who cares not for the reputation of the young maids who admire his good looks.' Her face was set in a determined fashion that almost scared Penelope. Or was it the cold harsh truth delivered within her words?

'I . . . I wouldn't!' Penelope was shocked by the accusation.

'You'd have no choice if a man forced himself on you. And you dipping in the water part-dressed . . . many would see it as an open invitation. Oh, don't deny it!'

Penelope looked down, shamefaced. 'I know, I've been stupid. I wanted to swim again, that was all.'

'You are a woman, not a child, and it's about time that you realised that you need to behave accordingly. Take that vexed look out of your eyes. Did he see you?' she persisted.

'No!' Penelope hoped she was not blushing. 'Not in the water.'

'Well, by God, I hope he did not see anything of you indecently out of it!' She shook her head. 'Come now, we have wasted enough time. We will get you back, but miss, please don't be so — excuse me for saying this bluntly, but as my mother would say to me — so bloody stupid again!'

Penelope sighed. She was utterly in the wrong, and to chastise or threaten this woman, who apparently had been sent to spy upon her activities by her wise and worldly father, was pointless. She would not be able to stop her without risking bringing about her own downfall. Like it or not, this servant had the upper hand. Penelope had had her swim, and nearly sunk in life as a consequence.

'So, are we to be friends, or am I to be the thorn in your side, Miss Penelope Rose?' The woman smiled at the pun.

'Oh, very well then, although that is far from an original jest,' Penelope replied. 'We shall have an understanding between us. But do not try to be high-handed with me.'

'No, miss, I knows me place. But I also know what it was to be young and foolish. I married for love against me folks' wishes, was disowned by them, and now here is me, a widow, with no one to look out for me in me middle years. I've no choice but to work to keep meself fed and harboured. So why would I want to make life any more difficult than it already is?' She looked at Penelope through watery eyes, but sniffed and cleared her throat.

'Very well, Esther, you shall have a more pleasant life and home with me. I shall make sure that I am more careful in what I choose to do and shall avoid childlike whims. As you correctly say, I am a woman. You will now be more than my personal maid; I shall call you my companion. A new dress that may be more suitable for the position must be found. Perhaps that way we can both live a little in a more enjoyable manner. But you must not refer to me in such a tone in front of Mother, for she will dismiss you without reference. There would be little I could do if she did so, for she would make sure none of her friends within the area would employ you.'

'Oh, I know she doesn't take no nonsense from the likes of me. My folk do from the likes of her. But it is nice to know at least you know me given name.' The woman smiled genuinely at her and her cheeks coloured slightly.

Penelope nodded at that, but saw Esther's eyes harden as she said the words referring to her mother. Penelope's mother was a formidable lady who had no wish to acknowledge servants as people. To her they were more like her pets, there for her to chastise at will and occasionally praise; she ignored their lives and needs, and hated them being negligent in their duties. However, Penelope did not. She watched the eyes of the silent bystanders who shared their home, and realised the family was being observed daily by them. Penelope liked this woman. She had nerve, a wealth of experience and the fact she was alone in life made Penelope warm to her. Penelope had often thought herself alone, but she now realised that what she actually was, was lonely.

4

They walked in silence until they neared the Hall. When Penelope glanced down at her new companion, Mrs Esther Cuthbertson, she looked tired and sad.

'Once again, I am sorry, Esther. I thank you for your advice and guidance. I shall heed your words. I behaved badly. Take your rest and I will see Mama.' She did not wait for a reply, but ran straight up the stairs in order to change and present herself in front of her mother.

However, in her rush she had not seen that a gig was parked up at the side of the Hall, whilst the horse was being unharnessed and allowed to refresh itself from the horse trough.

Esther Cuthbertson knew the vehicle very well. Her Henry had fixed its wheel only a year since. Now it passed by his small gravestone regularly, as he had been buried in the churchyard by the man who she held responsible for putting him there. Bonaparte's soldiers had not come to these shores to gloat over his bones, but the reverend had played his part. Bleakly had a fat belly and was partial to fine brandy, wines and cheeses from France. Oh the man had taste that overruled his conscience when it came to the matter of consuming, selling and hiding contraband. He had never allowed anything to come in the way of him acquiring his creature comforts and his supplies. She clenched her fists by her sides as she glared at the gig. It had done its share of moving contraband brought ashore on the flat sands of Ebton to his vicarage in the darker days of the war. Politics, he had claimed to the members of his flock who dabbled in smuggling, were not their problem or concern, they needed to pray that the just were served — and in his case he was unjustly served well. However, their wellbeing was their concern, and so he had helped to fund their resourcefulness.

Now the money had dried up from the trade as the taxes had eased, but his hands were dirty by association, and Esther hated the man. It was a strong word but, she thought, as her nails dug into her clenched palms, it was not too strong for her heart. Her Henry might never have died if he had not been sent off to war.

She glared at the vehicle as if it was the man who owned it. For her husband had refused to join in and be tarred with the rest of them. So, they had turned on him as an outcast in the village where he had grown from boy to man. Bleakly saw to it, coercing and whispering fear of betrayal in their ears. Henry had been taken for a drink, and then another, until he found himself forced into service. She had figured out how Bleakly had done it, for she knew that her Henry had too-suddenly decided to fight for his country. He was happy fighting the battle against those like Bleakly who profited from an illegal trade on his own shores. Someone must have realised and told on him. What could she do? A woman left alone to cope, and then to grieve, now she knew he was dead. For certainly he had died of his untreated wounds. So she would do what she needed to avenge her man, but not now — when the time was right.

She walked indoors. A companion. She liked the idea, as she did the promise of a new dress. That young miss may be a bit of a free spirit, but she liked her. For one of her kind, she rebelled, but today she had acted no better than a whore — a clean one, perhaps. She smiled. Esther thought of Penelope's father. He really did not know just how much like him his daughter was. Would he be proud if he did, or would he beat some sense into her? She shook her head. She would never find out because she was not about to tell on the lass. It suited her purpose to be Penelope's companion, and the lass was very indebted.

5

'Mama! I heard that you are returned.' Penelope had quickly changed her dress and brushed out her hair, arranging it simply in a plait coiled in a soft bun, and wrapping a finer plait around her head, finished off with a few natural golden curls hanging loose. It was easy and quick for her to pin it up herself. Her discarded clothes were left in a heap on the floor as she hurried to appear to her mother before her absence was noticed, or maids were sent to find her.

'Where have you been? Without being too dramatic, I nearly fell prostrate in the street! Can you imagine how embarrassing that would have been? Thank goodness I was saved by a messenger of God's own people.' She fluttered her fan in front of her.

'A messenger from God?' Penelope

repeated, wondering if her mother had in fact fallen on her head. For, without sounding too 'dramatic', she was surely being so.

'Yes! I am truly blessed, at least with his ministers if not with my own daughter's caring presence. I am returned here safely. Now the Reverend Bleakly is downstairs awaiting me. I do hope he finds Cook's offerings sufficient to keep him comfortable whilst I have been having my hair redone.' She patted the back of her tightly pinned-up greying locks, with regimented curls pressed to her hairline.

Penelope pressed her lips firmly together, as she was sure that Bleakly's lips were happily devouring cakes in her father's house whilst he was elsewhere. So he was the ministering angel — a fallen one, she mused, if her father's comments on the man to his friends were correct. She had no reason to doubt them. She had heard most of them sitting at the top of the servants' stairs near his study, a good listening place.

'Your father had to stay in town, of course. Never let it be said that a poor female's weaker state, even that of his wife, should come before his business affairs.' She sniffed.

'I am sure he knows you are in good hands — if you have told him what happened?' Penelope queried.

'How could I when I was fainting!' she snapped.

So her father was none the wiser as to what his wife was doing. 'He certainly would not have realised that the reverend would be calling this afternoon . . . ' She let her words hang in the air between them as they stared at each other.

'Penelope, someone in the house has to have the talent of the diplomat, or heaven knows where we would be living. If it was up to your father, it would no doubt be in some hovel in the woodland, like the estate hermit — he could be at one with nature and would only offend the squirrels and God directly.' She shook her head delicately, apparently not wanting to disturb her carefully placed greying curls.

'We do not have a hermit, Mama,' Penelope said innocently, but caught the all-too-familiar look of vexation that her mother shot her.

'I was speaking rhetorically,' she said. 'Although fashionable establishments do have, I am assured.' She walked over to the door. 'You will accompany me.'

'Will I? Must I?' Penelope said without vetting her words first.

'Yes, indeed you must. I have heard that his son Mr Lucas Bleakly is returned from Oxbridge studies, and I would have you meet him,' she replied.

'No!' Penelope snapped out the word before she thought better of it and instantly flinched. Her defiance would ensure that her mother would insist that she did. Damnation! Would she never learn? Penelope berated herself.

'Yes, you will! There are few enough eligible bachelors in these parts and your father will not hear of you going into Ripon for the season, so I must intervene. He may not approve of the father, but the son I understand is in line to inherit from his uncle also. He was a Bishop and married well. His only son was killed at Trafalgar — poor thing. Still, that leaves Lucas the next in line to inherit the estate. So do not look down on the poor son of a preacher, as I assure you he is like a golden nugget as yet undiscovered.' She leaned closer to Penelope and whispered, 'Although, I have heard there are moves afoot from the Hendersons of Beckton; they may know of his fortune.' She sniffed. 'Have you been washing again? This weather may be uncomfortable, but you cannot run the maids ragged ferrying pails of water up and downstairs all day for you. Besides, it is no good, it will bring on the vapours and chills.'

'No, Mama, I have not, just a quick rinse,' Penelope said thinking that if she knew she had swum in an open pool, her mother would have her wrapped up and kept in a stuffy room for a week in case the 'vapours and chills' took hold. Penelope opened the door reluctantly, following on behind her mother. She trembled inside at the thought of having to sit next to — or even opposite — the smug face of Mr Lucas Bleakly at a dinner table. Her father would be silently fuming that he had been invited, and if the reverend and his wife were there too, the air would crackle with tension and unsaid accusations by both parties. It would be tense, all waiting for the spark that would ignite yet another row between Sebastian Rose and Willis Bleakly. Mrs Bleakly and her mama both would want the evening to go well and would make small talk, safe talk, whilst discreetly watching her and Lucas become better acquainted. How in the midst of such a charade could she join in? Every time his eyes looked at her, she would feel half naked in his presence, for he had seen her almost so, and wet to her skin. Penelope felt her colour heighten as her cheeks burned with guilt — and another sensation that she was finding hard to acknowledge. Somewhere deep inside that shame there was also a glimmer of excitement, for she had felt so alive. How could she refuse such a meeting?

'Penelope! Stop daydreaming, girl! Go down and announce my imminent arrival to Reverend Bleakly and I will arrive calm, as a hostess should do.' She straightened her back and held her head high.

For a moment, and it was a very brief moment, it occurred to Penelope that the way her mother was behaving demonstrated she too was feeling more than she ought. But that was ludicrous; this was fat old Bleakly, not his handsome son. Stopping her thoughts there, Penelope smiled.

'Yes, Mama,' she replied and began skipping down the stairs two at a time, biting her lower lip as she acknowledged just how handsome she thought the dark-haired Lucas Bleakly to be, with that accusing yet humourous glint in those equally dark brown eyes.

'Penelope.' The voice stopped her mid-step. 'Decorum, girl, decorum!'

'Yes, Mama, of course.' Penelope walked with her head held high, her shoulders and her back straight, down the remaining stairs. She would look over him and through him. He was her father's nemesis and should not step foot within their home, but Mama was ever the diplomat and worrier of what the gossips would make of her if they refused to entertain him. A thought occurred to her. If her father had forewarning of what her mother was planning for a union between her and Lucas, he would surely step in and stop her plans before she acted upon them at all. Yes, that was it. She would tell her father as soon as she saw him.

She neared the bottom step. Perhaps Mr Lucas Bleakly had fallen for Miss Henderson as Mrs Bleakly also wished. He did not seem keen on the notion, but then Penelope had distracted him.

No, the future was going to be bright. But an image of that handsome face regaling his afternoon's experience to the two impressionable women in order to gain their favour crossed her mind. She swallowed and tried to calm herself. She surely had to have more faith in the man than that — but why?

6

'Reverend Bleakly, my mama will be here very shortly. I hope you are well.' Penelope smiled through gritted teeth as he stood up, pulling a napkin from his neck and dropping it on a plate of crumbs on the table at his side.

'Ah, Penelope, how well you look,' he said, but then his attention passed over her as her mama made her entrance. 'Oh, if I may say so, you could be taken for sisters!' He took her mother's hand and gently touched it with his own.

Penelope cringed. It was such a weak, half-hearted gesture, like the man himself, she mused.

'You are too kind, sir,' her mother replied, and gestured that they should sit on the two settees that faced each other by the ornately plastered mantelpiece of the fire surrounds.

Penelope sat stiff like the unmoving

plaster and the cupids that adorned it. The only arrows she wished to shoot, though, were not of love.

'I am here on a mission of mercy,' he began. He licked his lips to scoop up a few escaping crumbs.

Penelope's smile was fixed. *He wants money again*, she thought. Why, with all his wealth, was he always wanting something?

'Whatever is it?' her mother asked with her 'caring' expression carefully filling her lined face.

'It is, well, quite personal,' he said, and coyly placed his head slightly on one side. His oily grey hair touched the dark fabric of his jacket, but his eyes never left her mother's face. They were too small, thought Penelope, and grey: lacking colour and strength.

'My dear sir, you must unburden yourself.' Her mother was practically on the edge of her seat.

Penelope saw her mother side-glance at her, but knew better than to speak or move at this point. However, her attention was also hanging upon the good reverend's words.

'I find myself at a loss as to what to do with Lucas.' He looked down momentarily.

Now, that was one confession that Penelope had not expected. He definitely had her attention. What had Lucas been up to? she wondered. Surely nothing more daring or foolish than *her* exploits!

'In what way?' her mother said compassionately, as if she was encouraging him like a bee to nectar to let her savour the truth.

For once her mother had taken the very thoughts from her mind and vocalised them.

'In the manner that, as a young, eligible and much-sought-after young man, he is being distracted from his true vocation.' He now sat forward and stared at her mother directly.

Penelope now felt very uneasy. She almost felt as though she should not be there, which did not seem correct at all.

'Does he have a 'vocation'?' Penelope asked, and saw that her mother was now casting her a warning glance. This was a conversation she should not interrupt.

'Oh, but he does. He just does not realise it yet. He is a very caring boy, who has had his head turned by more troubled characters. I would have him set back on a true path,' Bleakly explained in a manner that sounded sincere.

'Penelope, dear, I think you should go and find out what Cuthbertson is doing.' Her mother turned to her after she caught the reverend fidgeting and glancing in her direction.

'Exactly the sort of character I would shield my boy from. Henry Cuthbertson was a disreputable fellow, God rest his soul.' He glanced upwards. 'I think you are showing more Christian charity than his widow deserves by housing her here.'

Penelope watched his jowls wobble and thought of a bulldog. Not a very friendly one.

'Henry is dead. He served his country and died of his festering wounds. That is a horrible death, and his widow would have had to throw herself on the mercy of the parish poor laws if she had not been taken on by my father as an act of charity, but she does good work to earn her keep,' Penelope said, feeling oddly defensive of her new companion.

Her mother gasped at her bluntness.

'Point proved, I think, Mrs Rose.' The reverend stared at her. 'What the girl says may have a jot of truth within it, but the Cuthbertsons stir up passion and troubles. You mark my word, the Devil will have his way. I would suggest that Miss Penelope does not spend too much time in the woman's company if such forthright notions are filling her head.' He sat back.

'I do not spend my days listening to the grievances or tittle-tattle of the servants, sir. However, in order to try and educate her into a more civilised role, she is my companion and maid. I believe her harmless enough. The loss of Henry has been hard for her and left her quite melancholy and dispirited. Excellent qualities for a quiet companion.'

He stared at her. 'You have your father's gift of oratory, my dear. What a shame you could not join the clergy. However, perhaps a spell in a convent might give you more time to think and develop your ideas further.'

'Run along, Penelope. Find the woman and make sure she is kept busy. Idle hands, you understand.' Her mother acted quickly as Bleakly and Penelope stared at one another.

'Yes, Mama,' she replied and acknowledged Reverend Bleakly with a slight nod of her head as she stood and willingly left. A convent, indeed!

She opened the door, and closed it too quickly so that her new 'companion' could not be seen snooping on the other side of it.

Penelope glared at her and mouthed, *What do you think you are doing?*

53

Cuthbertson's reply was simple. *Listening!* She quickly took up her position by the slightly ajar doors and continued.

'You can't!' Penelope whispered, hardly audible.

'Yes, we can!'

Penelope was about to protest when she realised that she would love to know what Bleakly was up to with her mother, and so leaned over Cuthbertson's stooped figure in order to listen also.

7

'Eavesdroppers rarely hear good things of themselves . . . ' Her father's voice gave both women a start as he entered the hall.

'Father,' Penelope said as she walked guiltily away from the door. 'Esther, go and tell Cook that Father needs refreshments,' she ordered.

The woman dipped a curtsey and scuttled away down the servants' corridor to the kitchen. Her father smiled and looked at Penelope. '"Esther"? So we are getting on well with the servants, are we? So well that you are now partners in some sort of subterfuge.' He raised both eyebrows.

'Yes,' she said, and took his arm to lead him away from the door. 'You knew we would. Which is why Esther is now my companion, who will need a new dress to suit her position.

However, Mama is talking to Reverend Bleakly, who rescued her from town when she nearly fainted this morning.' Penelope watched the smile fade from both his eyes and his mouth as he took in her words.

'So why is he still here?' Her father almost snapped out the question.

'Well, it appears that young Mr Lucas Bleakly . . .'

'He is not that young, Penny,' he remarked.

She smiled as she always did when he used his pet name for her. Her mother forbade him to utter it within her or anyone else's hearing, as it sounded too common to her. Penelope suspected that the remark had actually hidden a tinge of jealousy, as father and daughter had always been so happy and comfortable in each other's company.

'Well, perhaps not, but he is apparently being wilful and does not seem disposed to do his father's bidding and join the church, or marry into a family of their choosing.' Penelope saw the look of bemusement and annoyance cross her father's face.

'What has this got to do with us?' he asked, becoming agitated. He obviously wanted to break up her mother's little tête-à-tête. He might not approve of her eavesdropping, but was interested in what she had heard.

'Well, he is seeking Mama's guidance . . . but Father — she has already said that she would like me to show interest in Mr Lucas Bleakly as he will inherit well.' Penelope looked innocently up into his sky-blue eyes and omitted to pass on the remark about sending her to a convent. She did not want to put Bleakly's suggestion into her father's mind. If he found out about her dip in the pool this morning, she would find herself sent to repent in a convent on some remote island, serving a penance until his temper cooled, like her body had as the water had caressed it. She had to subdue the urge to grin at the memory.

'I knew the man was a jackass . . . but

to ask your mother's advice on such an issue! If Lucas Bleakly has defied his father, then he must have a spine as well as been blessed with enough gumption to know his own mind. Perhaps I should meet the man. Come, it is time I broke up this ill-advised meeting and found out how my wife ails.' He did not wait for a response, but strode purposefully into the drawing room, where two startled faces turned and stared at him as if a ghost had entered.

'My dear, how do you fare?' He looked at his wife's high colour as she stood up immediately.

'Sebastian, Reverend Bleakly rescued me. This heat, it is the very devil, and I could barely stand to admire the hat display in the bay window.' She dabbed at her forehead with her laced kerchief.

'Well, we must let you rest then.' Penelope watched as he turned to Bleakly and, with a stony smile upon his face, outstretched a hand. It was not an offer to shake the other man's hand, but held flat merely to gesture toward the door. 'Come, Reverend, we have detained you long enough. I am sure your parish is missing you. I have had the horse reharnessed and shall see you to your gig. Penelope, escort your mother to her room. Too much excitement is no good on a day like this, she must rest. The heat is truly intolerable. Shall we?' He stepped back making room for Reverend Bleakly to pass before him.

The man appeared flustered but, although he glanced at Penelope's mother, there was nothing he could say, or do, but obey her husband's request and leave. It was polite yet bordering brusque, but it was undeniably clear.

'I thought Reverend Bleakly should stay for dinner after all he has done, and with the heat and everything . . . ' Her mother looked sheepishly at her father, but he merely shook his head.

'We must not be so selfish, my dear. I see he has already partaken today.' He stared at the tray upon which was a plate covered in crumbs and his discarded napkin. The empty tea cup was testament to the man's thirst having been sated also. 'You are not at your best. No, Reverend, please return on Friday as your schedule allows, and bring your lovely wife with you. I understand young Lucas has returned to you. I would enjoy knowing the man he has become. Bring him also.' His mouth smiled, but Penelope knew his eyes did not.

Whether Bleakly knew this, or not, he seemed pleased. Penelope watched an uncertain look exchange between both people, but it was Reverend Bleakly who broke the surprised silence.

'Very well, excellent; I would be delighted, as will my dear wife. Yes, young Lucas will enjoy it, I am sure, and Grace will think the idea divine.' He shook Sebastian's hand with renewed energy.

Her mother's face relaxed as the men left the room, but Penelope stood stock-still as the realisation of the position her father had unwittingly put her in became clear. Her nightmare was to become a reality. She would have to face the man who had stolen her clothes. Who had looked down on her wet form from above a rock and rebuked her as a naughty child. Her pride, already lost to him, would have to take another setback as he sat and gloated, or played with her like the cat with a mouse, should it please him to do so. For Penelope was all in the wrong, and she knew she could not tell a soul what the man knew. She blinked and held her eyes closed a moment as she said a quiet prayer in case Lucas should decide it an excellent opportunity to destroy her.

'Are you ill, girl?' Her mother's sharp words jolted her out of her trance.

'The heat, Mama; it is too much.'

'Oh dear, if you find it so then think for a moment of your poor mother. So stop dallying and feeling sorry for yourself and see me to my room. I have much to think on, whereas you are a girl with empty-headed notions who has not the good manners to keep her mouth shut in the company of her elders and betters.'

When her mother stopped for breath she literally had to gulp some in, and so Penelope linked arms with her and saw that beads of perspiration had formed upon her brow and her top lip. Despite the heat, she looked pale. Penelope realised then that her mother had not been feigning a faint for attention, but genuinely had felt unwell.

'Esther!' she shouted, and her companion arrived. 'Help me get Mama to bed, and then ask Father to send immediately for Dr Simmons.'

'Don't fuss, girl,' her mother said breathlessly, 'I will be fine, these turns pass.' As she spoke, she winced.

The moment she was in her bed-chamber, the message was dispatched to fetch the doctor, and the housemaid was sent up to attend her mother. It was not long before she was abed, and Penelope insisted the windows be opened wide, despite the protestations of her sleepy mother.

'Bring cooled water and cloths. I want to cool her down. She needs to breathe easily. Tell Father to come as soon as the doctor has been sent for.'

Penelope was doing all this by instinct, but that instinct was telling her loud and clear that something unnatural was happening to her Mama.

'Perhaps you were too quick to dispel with the reverend's services,' her mother quipped, and closed her eyes.

Penelope stared at her still form, breathing shallowly, and prayed — for once, sincerely — that they had not been. This woman was not close to her as a mother should be, but she was still her parent, and Penelope respected her as such — even if she doubted if her father did, or ever had. Theirs was a matched marriage, and that was why Penelope wanted only to marry for love — but did her father understand that? Could he, or was his heart hardened against the notion of a daughter having her own preferences in the matter? Would he expect her to obey him and marry a man he picked out for her? She winced at the thought, but realised how much her fate was not in her own hands.

8

'Father, have you sent for the doctor?' Penelope asked as she met him on the landing, once her mother's temperature seemed cooler and she was breathing easier.

'Yes, she is just making a fuss again!' he said, looking distracted, as if he was still thinking about Bleakly. 'The woman will make a drama out of anything.' He then stared at her as she sighed deeply. 'Do not please become her puppet and fall for her ways, Penny. She seeks attention always.'

'No, Father, she looked genuinely ill: grey of pallor, and with beads of perspiration forming on her lip. I believe she is really sick. Some things you cannot pretend.'

'Is it any wonder I do not believe her so easily when she insists on wearing full corset in this weather!' he snapped.

'Who is she trying to impress, anyway?' He made a sweeping gesture with his arm as if he was trying to lift her mood.

Then Penelope gasped, but with ease he took her hand in his. 'I will see her,' he said and smiled. 'Yes, girl, I have sent for the doctor. Do not look too shocked at my remarks. When in the house, Penny, you could remove your corset too; just whilst the heat is so bad. No one would know.' He winked at her. 'And now, to appease your concern, I will see the invalid has everything her heart desires.'

Penelope did not answer. His manner was cold. Not to her, but to his wife. Her heart did not desire anything; her heart needed a doctor to look at her, that Penelope was sure of. Then she cringed with guilt; for, had he only known that she had divested of far more than her corset — and outside the Hall, too — he would not be holding her hand and thinking her shocked so easily. It was his manner that surprised her, though. Although why it should, she knew not; for, other than polite endearments, she could not recall any genuine show of affection between him and her mother. Penelope's heart, troubled as it was with her own situation of facing Mr Lucas Bleakly, now had a more grave concern. Her mother was ill, and she seemed to be the only one who realised it or genuinely cared. That made her incredibly sad for the woman who had brought her into this world, and for the father she adored, but who clearly did not love his wife.

*   *   *

Sebastian entered the bedchamber. His mouth curled into an ironic smile as he did. His wife was abed, and he was allowed in because she could not voice her disapproval. His bitterness had shown to Penelope, which was something that he had promised himself would never happen. However, his wife talking to Bleakly behind his back was yet another one of her betrayals. She did not know loyalty. She knew how to live a lie and how to be the lady of his Hall, his fine home, but had no idea or inclination to be a woman in a man's bed — well, not her husband's.

She was breathing shallowly, but he registered that she was breathing still, and was quite shocked to realise that with that recognition a feeling of disappointment swept through him.

He stepped forward and ran his finger gently along the back of her hand. It was amazingly young, still having not worked. Gloves had protected it from the sun. He had loved her once, desired her, longed to see her; but now . . .

'Sebastian,' she whispered, and her lids opened.

'Yes, dear. Penelope thinks you are genuinely ill,' he said quietly, as if reflecting upon his own words.

'And you do not?' Her voice was a little clearer, yet lacked the volume to deliver the snapped retort back at him as she would have most likely wanted to.

'I do not know, my dear. You see, Penny does not know how many times you have feigned headaches, backaches, agues, spasms — anything to keep me at arm's length.' His words, unspoken for years drifted off his tongue into the air between them. He was not surprised that watery eyes stared back at him, because he would have expected nothing less. If she was genuinely ill then this time, she would surely be as dramatic as she could to try and make him suffer. But he would not. Sebastian thought he was immune to her hurtful ways.

'Why say such horrid things to me now, of all times?' she croaked the words. 'It is too cruel,' she added in little more than a whisper.

'No, my dear, it is only the truth.'

9

When Penelope entered the room after her father stormed out, it was to find her mother sobbing into the pillow. She was unusually unaware of Penelope's presence, which instantly told her that the tears and heartache were genuine.

'Whatever is it, Mama?' she asked, feeling strange in the role of comforter.

'Your father is so cruel,' she muttered. 'You only see his kind side, but he is a man who knows only his own will and cannot fathom how any woman can, or should, stand against him. The day you cross that will of his, child, you will understand.' She looked at Penelope and lifted her hand in a slow, laboured movement to stroke her daughter's cheek. 'You are so like him.'

Penelope recoiled, for she took the woman's meaning to be that she too was selfish and cruel.

'You are ill, Mama, you do not know what you say.' Penelope did not want the conversation to deepen or become more insulting. Her mother was in no position to fight back, and Penelope did not want to prove her poorly-chosen words correct by rounding on a weakened woman. 'The doctor will be here soon.' She stood up.

'See, you do not hear what you wish to, so you too will desert me and also storm off. Am I to die here alone?' Her eyes were seemingly pleading with Penelope to understand her plight, but she could not, or did not want to. It was always her mother who fussed about and complained, who was moody, and who rebuked . . . not her father. He went calmly about his business and brought sunshine back into the house with his warm smile and attitude.

'Please, stop saying such words, Mama, and calm your nerves.' Penelope spoke gently and sat back down. 'It is you who say such cruel things, Mama. I only want you well again and yet you always seek to hurt me with criticisms of me and Papa.' Penelope kept an even tone to her words to try and make her mother see that they were not bad people, but that she was too sensitive and, well . . . temperamental.

'Is that what you think of me?' She shook her head a little, winced, breathed deeply and closed her eyes. 'I only want you to understand me. To understand my plight and see your father afresh — but how can you? You are only a girl!' She sniffed. 'He will marry you off to a Bleakly if he can.'

'Surely not! He does not even like Reverend Bleakly, let alone know his son.'

'Ha! He would do it to spite Willis, and to guarantee an heir for his Hall. I have served it well over the many years I have been trapped here, and now it will be for you to carry on and pick up the mantle. Lucas Bleakly would serve his purpose well. He does not like his father either, rebels at every turn; he will have money, but no hall of his own to look after — or any responsibilities, if he does not go into the clergy — and therefore he will be free to take over here when that time comes.'

'But I do not know, let alone love, Mr Lucas Bleakly!' Penelope said quietly, trying to absorb these differing viewpoints. Shockingly, she was actually beginning to doubt her father. Which of her parents was speaking the truth?

'What has either love or knowledge to do with it? If your father decides upon your future and the Bleaklys are willing, he will have you married off by the end of the season. He will have it announced and so trap the lad into it. Once printed in the press, Lucas will not be able to default on his promise without losing his good name, and possibly a part of his inheritance. Either way, your father gets his wish, and smites Willis into the bargain!' She coughed and struggled for breath. Her agitation had grown as her words poured out in a croaky but deliberate fashion.

Penelope stroked her back gently as she sat forward, then rested her mother carefully against the pillow. 'But it is what you want, isn't it?' she asked gently.

'I want a good match for you, yes — but I would have you loved as a wife should be. Willis tells me that Lucas has kept bad company, cards and the like, at private clubs, but at heart he is a good boy. He wanted you to nurture him back to what Willis sees as his calling.' She sighed deeply and her eyes fluttered open slightly finding Penelope's troubled face.

'But Reverend Bleakly does not like me, Mama,' she replied, carefully pondering the ease with which her mother used his Christian name.

'He does not approve of that streak of your father's disrespectful nature that shows itself occasionally, but he has always found you a good-natured and able girl. It is this he feels Lucas would nurture in you, as you would keep him away from the gaming tables

74

and . . . wilful women.'

Penelope stared at her. 'Wilful women?' she questioned.

'Yes, well, women who would . . . '

There was a knock on the door. It opened and Esther walked in with the doctor. Her father loitered near the doorway, as if half-decided to stay and half to go. He was normally such a determined man that indecision, Penelope thought, did not suit him at all.

'Should we wait downstairs, Doctor?' Penelope asked.

'Please, can she stay?' Her mother's feeble request was granted as the doctor nodded and her husband retreated.

It was a cursory examination, but one that involved her mother trying to breathe deeply. The doctor looked at her clammy skin and insisted that she was dried, changed and kept warm. The windows were shut. Penelope could not imagine how anybody could possibly be anything other than warm on such a day, although evening would be soon upon them and the cool air would arrive with it.

'You should be bled to get your humours back in balance, Mrs Rose,' Dr Simmons said and opened his bag.

'But she is already so pale.' Penelope was appalled at such an idea, and for once her mother was in complete agreement.

'I will not be bled, sir. For I have little enough to spare.' She tried to smile.

'My dear lady, I am the doctor, and I am sure that your husband would want me to prescribe a treatment as I see fit,' he admonished.

'Perhaps, but as Mother has already had a difficult day, you could let her rest this evening and visit us again in a day or so, when her nerves are calmer and her heart stronger,' Penelope offered.

'Yes, yes that would be agreeable. I am so tired. If it is necessary then please arrange it in a day or so,' she said and closed her eyes.

'Very well,' he said. 'You must rest for a few days then. You have been overdoing it and should allow yourself time to gather your energy again. This heat is draining on ladies of a certain maturity, so I will leave something for you to help you sleep. Then when I return on Friday, if there is no improvement, I will arrange for the bleeding process to begin.'

'Thank you, Dr Simmons,' Penelope said, as Esther showed him out.

'Bleeding indeed! I have no good humour on the subject at all. I will not abide it! Since when does cutting someone heal them? Utter nonsense!' Her mother's voice was full of its normal vexation.

'You should rest,' Penelope said. 'Then you will not need bleeding and you can look forward to a dinner party instead. But if it is too much, then Father can cancel or postpone the invitation,' Penelope said, trying to hide her enthusiasm for the idea. She wanted it postponed indefinitely.

'I will, but think on what I have said, Penelope. Either way, you should give Lucas a chance.'

Penelope nodded, but as she left the room, she knew they were all to be disappointed — because no respectable man would give *her* 'a chance' after seeing her swim so brazenly in the pool. She would have to be humble, and hope that he would behave like an honourable man to a woman who had shown herself not to be.

10

Penelope saw her father bid Dr Simmons goodbye in the hallway. He was shaking the man's hand firmly and patting him on his back as if he had done a good job. Penelope wondered why, when the man had spent no more than five minutes in her mother's company.

'Well, if she is not out of bed and about as normal by the end of the week, I will send my boy with a message, so that you can tell the surgeon you recommended he can bleed her. It is time she had some good humours in her.' Her father smiled and the doctor laughed.

'They may be the weaker sex, but mention surgical treatment and their strength returns. I will be surprised if she is not sat opposite you at the dinner table on Friday evening. However, a good bleeding is most refreshing; my own father swore by it. In the meantime, she may as well sleep and get her rest. Goodbye, Sebastian.' He replaced his tall hat and left in his own coach.

Penelope's hands curled into fists as her father watched the doctor go. Simmons was an educated man. He had a profession that people respected, and discreetly paid him sufficient to own a coach. Dr Simmons dined at the best tables, yet he could not determine when a woman was genuinely ailing. He visited, prescribed — and yet it was only the surgeon and apothecary who actually did anything.

Her father turned around and saw her staring at him. 'What is it, Penny?' he asked.

'She is genuinely ill, Father. It is no laughing matter.' Penelope stepped forward toward him, but he did not lift his arms to her in a comforting gesture. Instead, he raised a finger as he made his next point.

'Then she should have agreed to his suggested treatment.' He shrugged. 'If your mama cannot organise the menu for our guests on Friday, then you will put your admirable skills to use. Speak to Cook and see what she recommends when you organise your mama's meals.'

Penelope blinked when he walked into his study as if there was no more to be said or done. Dinner was a quiet affair, and the evening dragged on. Her father refused to discuss her mother. Instead, he left the table early as he said he had letters to write. Penelope returned to her mother's bedside three times before she turned in.

★   ★   ★

The next morning, her mother still slumbered. Was the medicine perhaps too strong? Penelope wondered, as her shallow breaths laboured on.

'We best get some of Cook's chicken broth for her. I reckon we'd do her better than them menfolk, for all their education.' Esther smiled, but she meant her words.

Penelope glanced down at Esther, who had appeared at her side. 'Can you organise it for me? I need to get some fresh air and to think.' Penelope looked at her, imploring her not to challenge her on this.

'Yes, miss, I can, but please do not go beyond the gardens. We don't want you in trouble again; and besides, she sleeps now, but when she wakes you should be near. You are right, I fear. She is unwell.'

Penelope nodded and collected her walking coat and hat. By the time she stepped outside into the morning air, her father had already left. His room looked as if he had not slept in it.

She knew she should stay within the gardens, but she took a path out of the side of the wall and up a steep bank towards the moor road. It was wild and fresh there. She could see for miles and she wanted to be alone. She would have been, if not for a rider who was heading along the track towards the Hall.

'Please,' she muttered, 'do not let it be Reverend Bleakly!' How would it appear if she was out gallivanting when her mother lay ill abed? As he neared, it was apparent that the rider was younger and held good posture. It was not Reverend Bleakly, but Mr Lucas Bleakly.

'Damnation!' she whispered under her breath. How would it look to him? Could she fall even lower in his estimation? She was out on her own when she was needed in the Hall.

She turned her back to him, and was about to make her way back off the track and down into the Hall's grounds again, when his voice bellowed over the purple of the heather and begged her to stop and wait for him.

He pulled in the horse's reins as he approached and dismounted by her side. This was not the time to admire his athletic ability, but the man was a competent rider and knew how to dismount in style. However, his manner was not of someone who was out to impress, but instead his face showed genuine concern. 'Miss Rose, please wait. I wish to talk with you,' he said, as he stepped near to her.

She looked up into his fresh, yet mature face. How could she say she had no wish to talk with him — especially as something deep down inside her was telling her that simply was not true?

'I cannot stay, sir. I only wished to refresh my lungs and am needed back at the Hall . . . My mother . . . she is unwell.' As she spoke he was nodding.

'Yes, I know. I met Dr Simmons last night, and he told me she was melancholic and needed to be shocked out of it.'

His indelicate words tore at Penelope's heart. 'How dare he!' she snapped. 'My mother is ill, not 'melancholic', and if he cannot see that 'snapping her out of it' could break her heart — literally — then he should not be in the position he so proudly flaunts!'

She stepped back, amazed at the strength of her own words.

'I agree with you, Miss Penelope.' He stood before her, not a smile upon his face. He actually appeared to mean what he had said.

'You do?' she asked, anxious that this was not a trap that she had naively walked into.

'Yes.' He looked to the sky a moment. 'I will be honest with you, for you and I already share secrets, and that means we should trust each other.' He glanced back down at her.

Penelope's cheeks burned. She looked into his eyes: they did not shift their gaze anywhere but seemingly straight into her soul. 'Why?'

'Because I would have thought I had earned your trust. I have not told a soul of your little adventure. I merely sought to warn you and protect your good name. You have spirit, that is admirable, but you are now a beautiful woman and not a wilful child. The heat has subsided and cold weather will start coming in as the month progresses, so no more dips in the pool will be needed.' He tilted her chin up so that she could not look away from him.

'You do not intend to hold that over me, then?' she asked.

'No,' he smiled. 'To be honest, you beat me to it, for I was going there for the same reason.' He smiled at her.

'You are a man. You can.' She glared at him. He removed his hand.

'Now, that is the spirit I expect to see. You make a good point about the doctor, but Simmons is both the son and grandson of physicians. They bought their way into the trade. Their family makes a good living and frequently bad decisions.' He looked down at his boots for a minute as she took in his words.

'You cannot prove this, can you?' she asked.

'No, not yet, but one day I will. You see, I did not waste my time at university as Mother has indelicately hinted, and so started a rumour. I studied the subjects so I too became a doctor. But my father and mother are disappointed in me; because whereas I want to help the poor to find cures for cholera, typhoid, scarlet fever or even simple croup, they would have me preach to them from a pulpit, at a safe and respectable distance.' He sighed.

'So you did not nearly fail at university; instead, you succeeded in a different discipline.' Penelope smiled at him. He was a man who knew his mind and who cared.

'Can you help my mother? He wants to bleed her.' She swallowed. 'He has given her laudanum and she sleeps heavily. If she does not wake and get up, they will bleed her by the hand of the surgeon. I am so scared for her. My grandmother never recovered from such a wound as was inflicted upon her by a surgeon.'

She saw his look of anger or despair replaced by compassion.

'I will try, but tell me — is your father at home?' he asked.

'No, he left for town early,' she replied.

'Good. If I call, can you slip me up to her room so that I may see her, briefly?'

'Yes, I think so. But what if she wakes?'

'Then we are in trouble again. Or I will be. You will tell them I forced my way in to make my arrogant prognosis. They will believe that of me, I am sure.' He remounted and turned the horse back to the track.

'I will hurry, Lucas,' she said, as she made her way down to the Hall; but then, as she heard the words, 'Thank you, Penelope,' her heart, which had started the day feeling so heavy, experienced a surge of relief and hope.

11

Penelope entered the Hall and made her way to the morning room. She rang the servants' bell for Esther to come, but the woman was already there the moment Penelope's hat and coat were discarded on the back of a chair.

Her companion opened her mouth as if she was going to rebuke her mistress, but Penelope jumped in first. 'Is Mama awake, Esther?'

'No, but . . . ' She had picked up Penelope's coat and was draping it over her arm. The gesture was firm as she began to choose her words. Penelope was in too much of a rush to wait; besides, she wanted to make sure that Esther did not take the upper hand in their new situation. Penelope realised that her mother's failing health must have been the reason why she had not overruled her decision to have

Esther as her companion. In many ways, she was indeed unsuitable. Penelope needed to take control of things; her mother genuinely needed her.

'Never mind about any 'but's now. You can say your piece later. I am asking for your help,' Penelope said, as maturely as she could, but saw the glint in Esther's eye and thought better of adopting her mother's tone of ordering her to give it. 'What I mean is, it is an urgent situation and I would appreciate your help.' She saw the woman's eyebrows rise. The word 'Again?' was almost written on her lips, but Penelope ignored it — at least she now had her attention and interest.

'Mr Lucas Bleakly is about to arrive. When he does, I would like you to show him into the library,' Penelope said; and realised straight away, as Esther's eyes widened, that it must look as though she had just had another 'assignation' with the man this morning.

'Explain, miss, please?' Esther asked

politely, as her tongue settled inside her cheek.

'Well, you see, all is not as it seems with him. He is a physician, and that is why his mother and father are so angry with him. He did not do as they willed. He wants to help people and has turned his time at university to his own ends, instead of following his father's advice and preferences. So he knows of Dr Simmons' family . . . and their reputation.' The last statement was said directly so that its implication was not lost on Esther.

'Good heavens!' Esther snapped. 'And you found all this out — how and when, exactly?'

'Good heavens, indeed!' Penelope looked out of the window to see if there was any sign of Lucas riding down their long drive. There was not, but it gave her a chance to turn away from Esther's curious and knowing eyes. 'However, it is not for us to judge. I want you to make sure that . . . '

'Excuse me, miss, but how and when

did you discover all of this?'

Penelope glanced back. Esther had crossed her arms. The woman was infuriating in her persistence and doing.

'This morning . . . I . . .'

'Oh, you just happened to bump into him in the walled garden, I suppose? What was he doing, miss? Stealing the apples, like he did when he was a nipper?' She put her head on one side.

Penelope sighed. She owed Esther dearly for keeping her secret; otherwise, she would be tempted to dismiss her for insolence on the spot. Then she thought about her own readiness to do so, the dire implications it would have for this widow, and felt unusually ashamed that she could condemn a person to abject poverty because they vexed her. 'I do not have time for this, Esther. I walked further — I admit that — but what I said is true, and he will arrive shortly. I want you to take him to the library and make sure that the upstairs maid is sent downstairs before his arrival. You see, I want him to see Mama. I can take him up the servants' stairs from the library to the upper landing next to Papa's room. If she still sleeps, he can slip in and take a look at her — in my presence, I mean, and of course just a cursory assessment.'

'Are you mad, lass? If your father returns or anyone gets wind of this, it will go very badly. Let alone if your mother wakes . . . ' Her free hand now formed a fist that settled on her hip.

'Only a few minutes, Esther, to possibly save her life! Or do you wish to see her bled by a butcher of a surgeon when she is already weakened?' Penelope rounded on her companion, keeping her voice low and controlled as she did not want her words overheard.

'If this goes badly, you must take the full responsibility, lass, with your Mr Lucas.'

'Yes, agreed.' Penelope did not know how she felt about Mr Lucas being 'hers', but the notion had a pleasant ring to it.

'Thank you. And, miss, do not lie to

me again. You met him on the moor road. If you want Esther's help, you must trust her. Although why I should trust you and that whippersnapper of a young man, I have no idea. Physician, indeed! You had better tell me later just how well you do know him, for I cannot watch your back if half the time I don't know where it is.'

'Please, Esther . . . '

'Oh, very well. Go and check on your ma; send Sally down and I'll give her something to do in the kitchen dairy. When he comes, he'll go straight to the library, you fetch him up from there. But if your mama wakes, the Hall will shake with her screams, and no wonder.' Esther watched out of the window for Lucas to come into sight whilst Penelope made her way upstairs.

It felt the right thing to do, but Esther was correct. If it went badly, there would be no explanation she could give that would not bring down her father's fury on them both, and that would hardly do any good for her mother's situation.

Once Sally had disappeared to the kitchens, it was not long before Lucas arrived. Esther was as good as her word and showed him there without question to the library. Penelope saw him enter and opened the hidden servants' door wide, which gave him quite a start.

'Penelope, I fair thought your father was about to leap out of the very shelves at me!' He walked over to her briskly, showing that he too was anxious about their plan.

She was too nervous to smile. 'Come, Lucas, we must be quick. She is still asleep and her breath is shallow. Once you have seen her you must return here straight away. I will go down the main stairs and receive you in the morning room. That will give us time to discuss her situation and what should be done — in front of my companion who will be there, as is proper.'

'Your companion?' he asked, obviously not sure about involving the trust of another person.

'Yes, Esther Cuthbertson . . . '

'You trust her!' His face showed his surprise. She had forgotten the bad blood between his father and Henry Cuthbertson.

'Yes! You should not judge what you do not understand, and have only your father's accusations to go on. Now, should we?' She gestured to the passage behind her. 'If, that is, I am to discard the rumours about you and take you to my ailing mother on trust?'

'Ouch! You have a sharp, if justified, tongue. Show me the way; we can save debates for Cuthbertson's curious ears.' The line of his mouth betrayed a smile.

She did not respond, and instead led him quickly up the narrow stone staircase. She had never realised just how hard it must be for the servants to move around these parallel hidden passageways quietly — whilst carrying things, too — never disturbing the family's peace. The experience made her aware for the first time of another existence within her home that had continued on without her ever considering it. Somehow the thought disturbed her deeply.

They moved quickly to the door of her mother's bedchamber. She placed a finger to her lips and touched Lucas's arm so he would stay there whilst she slipped inside. Penelope tiptoed over to her mother's side. Convinced that her slumber was undisturbed, she returned quickly and opened the door, allowing him inside.

He made straight for the bed. 'She needs the windows opening in here, the place is airless.' He moved to her mother's side of the bed and placed the back of his hand upon her mother's brow.

Without waiting for a response from Penelope, he then found her wrist and held it lightly between his thumb and finger.

'Lucas . . . '

'Ssh . . . ' he said, as her mother's hand was raised.

Penelope was taken aback, but set

about opening two windows, allowing fresh air into the overbearing atmosphere within the room.

She watched him tuck her mother's wrist back under the covers. He then turned his attention to picking up the small bottle that was on the bedside table. He walked over to the window, wrapping the heavy curtain behind him so that he disappeared from view, and held the bottle up to the daylight. Penelope, curious, also slipped behind the drape and joined him. He was studying it and was reading the label.

'What is wrong, Lucas?' she asked.

He shook his head, then removed the stopper and sniffed the contents.

The glass was quite dark, so Penelope did not think he would have gleaned much from holding it up to the sun. However, he seemed satisfied with his inspection.

'You will pour two-thirds of this away, and then dilute the remaining fluid. Make sure that the level is as it is here.' He pointed to a place on the side of the vessel just above the label. 'This is no tincture for health: it is a drug that will guarantee she is in no fit state to rise before Simmons can claim more fees for having her bled. Then, that done, his prescriptive treatment will change. She will either rouse, and he will take all the credit for her strength and renewed energy; or, if the cut becomes infected, then the butcher he uses as his surgeon will make more coin at your father's financial expense and your mother's physical one by doing a 'corrective' further incision.' He passed the bottle to her and sighed. 'He is, I fear, not an honourable man.'

'But, despite what people have said about you, you are?' Penelope was huddled next to him. Her mouth had initially dropped open at such a declaration of Dr Simmons' lack of knowledge or care for her mother; but after the questions had slipped from her lips, he looked at her and raised one eyebrow.

'I fear you listen to the wrong sort of people.'

If what Lucas had said was correct, the man was a charlatan who must have harmed many people in his time practising as a physician. It made her blood boil that her father could not see it, and allowed him so near to her mother.

'But will she rouse even without this?' she whispered. She had unwittingly clenched the bottle within an angry fist. Penelope had realised that he had not answered her question about his honour, but she had registered a smile at the corners of his mouth when asked about it.

'I believe so. She is weak, as much through being drugged as her malaise; this results in a lack of nourishment, and I believe her heart is not as strong as it once was, but taking her life force — her blood — from her would be as to drain it away. I would, therefore, strongly recommend that the room is freshened. No more of this 'medicine' is to be given to her again until tonight, and then ensure that it is the much-weakened strain. Today she needs to eat warm broth and have plenty of fluids, little and often. Now, I think I should return to the library, Penelope.' His head was bent down towards her as they whispered in their curtain cocoon to each other. Penelope had been looking so intently into his eyes that she did not move at first when he finished speaking.

He quickly touched his lips to her forehead before turning around and stepping back into the dim light of the bedchamber.

Penelope hesitated for a moment, not knowing if that surprising gesture had been a half-attempted kiss, an accident, or a brush of affectionate reassurance. She quickly smiled at the delightful sensation, but then was filled with guilt as she remembered the reason for their inappropriate situation, so also spun out from behind the curtain to see the back of Lucas stationary in the room.

'You must return to the library, Lucas, before . . . '

Penelope followed the line of his gaze and swallowed, for sitting up in the bed was her mother. She appeared to look at Lucas and then straight at her daughter. Her white lace cap upon her head gave her an almost ethereal quality, especially with the white linen nightdress that covered her upper body above the coverlets.

'Penelope, what is the meaning of this?' Her voice sounded confused and a little feeble.

'Mama, how well you look!' Penelope said softly, and stood in front of Lucas, gesturing with her hand behind her back that he should continue on his journey out of the room. She moved up to the bed and blocked her mother's vision further. Penelope had realised that, although her mother was staring at them, the woman was sleepy and her eyes were not normally as keen as they once were in the dim light.

'Who else is here?' she asked, her

eyes scrunched up as she peered beyond Penelope, but Lucas had already slipped away.

'I will speak to Cook and have a tray brought in for you, Mama,' Penelope said, as she smoothed down the covers.

'Very well,' her mother replied without arguing. She closed her eyes again. Penelope left with the medicine in her skirt pocket and walked straight down the main staircase.

'Esther!' she shouted.

'Yes, ma'am,' Esther said. 'You have a visitor, Miss Penelope. Mr Bleakly is in the library.'

'Oh, really!' Penelope deliberately appeared a little flustered at the announcement. 'I will greet the reverend,' she replied, as Sally was standing just behind Esther.

'Yes, miss; only it is young Mr Lucas Bleakly, not the reverend,' she added.

'Sally, ask Cook to have some broth taken up to Mama, and stay with her to make sure she eats it. Esther, you will accompany me in the morning room, as

Father is not present; we will see what Mr Bleakly wants.'

'Yes, miss,' Sally replied and ran off about her tasks.

'I will go in, you fetch Lucas,' Penelope whispered, and walked into the morning room. She breathed deeply by the open window. How near a scrape that was! She smiled at how close Lucas had stood, and it pleased her; but how near her mother had come to finding them both in her bedchamber — that had scared her.

Penelope smiled again. Her days were normally long and quite boring, but of late she felt alive in a way she had not since she had been a daring and carefree child. However, she would do her best to keep her mother well, and so that had to be her first priority. All notions of Lucas had only to be focused on that matter — or so she told herself.

12

Esther opened the door and allowed Lucas to enter. Penelope saw such a contrast between the tall athletic build of Lucas and Esther's stocky, grey-haired figure.

'Your guest, miss,' she said boldly, as she shut the door behind them. She then walked over to her mistress's side and — without waiting for either Penelope or Lucas to speak, and in a voice that was more like her normal abrupt manner — said, 'Explain!'

'Do you normally allow your servants to be so bold?' Lucas's dark features looked most severe as he stared at Esther.

'My name is Mrs Esther Cuthbertson. You might remember my husband, Mr Henry Cuthbertson. He died saving this land of ours from Bonaparte, so I will speak as I see fit!'

'Esther, Lucas, please. Let us remember what we are about here. This is not a time to squabble over past misunderstandings. Mother needs our help.' She smiled and could see that the anger in Lucas's eyes was replaced by humour. But her words had not been chosen well, for she saw the expression upon Esther's face change.

'Misunderstandings! Aye, sorry to have been so slow to have realised that my Henry's removal from his homeland and his subsequent death were no more than a 'misunderstanding' between the Cuthbertsons and the Bleaklys!' She was about to storm out of the room.

'Esther, please . . . ' Penelope looked at Lucas for help, as she was lost for words.

'Mrs Cuthbertson, I have only heard of the tales of what transpired here from my father, and so will not have heard your account of what happened whilst I was away at boarding school. I was not a party to any of it, and so would ask that you keep that affair separate to the one that has brought me here today,' he said, his words calm; and she looked back at him and stopped.

Her eyes were moist and her cheeks flushed. However, she returned to Penelope's side.

'Well, you have shown more decency in them few words than your father has done in his lifetime here.' She then looked up at Penelope. 'So what's all this crawling around to your mother's room about, miss?'

Penelope had seen Lucas wince at the woman's words, but he did not rise to them, just merely stared at Penelope as if the conversation should be continued in another place at another time.

'Lucas thinks that Mama is sedated and does not need as much of the prescribed medicine as she has been given. She is weaker than she once was, but should return to good health.'

'Basically, Mrs Cuthbertson, the lady

needs a lighter diet; less heat, which will pass as the weather is already cooling down; and to avoid lifting heavier weights or exhausting herself. Gentle walks around the grounds would be beneficial in the fresh air.'

'Very well, but she isn't noted for lifting much,' she added.

'Nor should she be,' said Penelope sharply.

'Do you want some refreshments brought in? Or do you have to be going?' Esther was staring at Lucas. Penelope realised how bitter she was — but Esther had better harness that ill will, or her position could be jeopardised. She would have words with her companion later.

'I should be on my way,' Lucas replied.

'Surely a drink before you leave would be welcome,' Penelope offered.

Lucas hesitated.

'Oh, sit yourself down, I'll go and fetch it,' Esther snapped and stormed out.

'I apologise for her ill temper. I have never seen her like that before.' Penelope realised she had never given the woman much attention at all until her recent needy situation arose.

'I understand her husband was a good man. I cannot say with my hand on my heart, Penelope, that my own father has been, or is.' He stepped in front of her and stared into her eyes. With one finger he tucked a wayward curl of corn-coloured hair behind her ear. 'Forgive me for being so blunt and so forward. I find myself in a difficult situation. I am painted a shady character because, in a way, I betrayed my father's trust. Yet I did so because I believe I can genuinely help people. There is so much happening in the medical world. In France they have taken the science of pathology to a new place. Here they stick their heads in the sand, and their saws in the blood-soaked sawdust . . . oh, forgive me.' He stepped away.

'Why? Your words are filled with

passion and desire to do well, so what is there to forgive?' Penelope touched his hand so that he would turn back to face her.

'But you are an innocent young maid, and I talk of blood and . . . it is not fitting. Nor should I criticise my own father in front of you. What will you think of me?' he asked.

'That you are honest and refreshing. I stood wet and near-naked before you, and you wonder what I think of you? Surely, Lucas, it should be me who turns away in shame.'

He cupped the back of her delicate neck in one hand and stood close. 'Penelope, you are a vision of beauty, and I adore your spirit.' He bent his head so that his lips touched hers. Penelope's eyes closed as she savoured the moment of his tender kiss. Her heartbeat seemed to quicken. All too soon, their lips parted and he stepped back. Their eyes stared into each other's as silence filled the gap between them until Penelope spoke.

'You are a rebel, sir, but a good-hearted one.'

'And you, Miss Penelope, are my rose.' He smiled at her blushes, when the door was flung open and Esther returned with the maid carrying the tray.

'Set it down there, Sally,' she ordered.

When the maid left, Esther looked from one to the other of them. 'So, are both your folks agreed that you'd make a good match, or has Cook got it all wrong?'

'Go and check on Mama!' Penelope ordered.

Esther chuckled, dipped a curtsy. 'Yes, miss,' she said innocently, and left them alone again.

'Has Cook got it wrong, Penelope?' Lucas asked as he sipped his tea.

'We hardly know each other . . . and yet, we do seem destined in some way to . . .'

The door opened as Esther's head and shoulders appeared. 'Your father's

111

just riding up the drive, full pelt.'

'Thank you, Esther. You had best come back in here.'

Penelope was seated on one sofa by the fireside, and Lucas on the opposite one. Esther was by the table with the tray so that she could serve, yet ensure that Penelope was not compromised by being in the room on her own with Lucas. The thought made her smile. This was like a game of charades. She desperately wanted to ride with him and continue their conversation in the open grounds of the estate, but she would need her father's permission for that. If she was honest, she would love to swim with him, and . . .

Her father entered. 'Good morning, Lucas! Sally has told me you visit. I hope all is well at the vicarage?' He came over and shook Lucas's hand before sitting down next to him. His eyes had scanned the room as he walked over.

'Perfectly, sir,' Lucas explained. 'I was riding by and thought I would call and express my thanks for your kind dinner invitation. Mother is most looking forward to it and I am pleased to know that your good lady wife is recovering swiftly.' He smiled and was being most pleasant.

'Of course it is always good to have visitors, especially such well-educated ones as yourself.' Her father's words were somehow guarded.

Penelope could sense something was amiss, but could not quite understand what it was.

'You flatter me, sir,' Lucas said and glanced curiously at Penelope.

'I mean, why else would a young man of learning be in my wife's bedchamber?' Her father looked at Lucas and then at Penelope, his raised eyebrows revealing he knew fine well what they had done. But how? Penelope wondered.

Esther stood up.

'Sit down, woman,' her father ordered, and Esther flopped back into the chair.

'If you stand to the light and that

light is provided by a window, do you not realise that anyone who was out riding on the estate within vision could see the two of you as clear as day as you connive together? Where is your intelligence in that? Well, which one is going to explain first?'

13

'Father, we acted in Mama's best interests,' Penelope said.

'I take full responsibility,' Lucas began. 'I suggested that I do a cursory examination of Mrs Rose, sir . . . '

'Without my knowledge or consent, you entered my wife's bedchamber!' Her father snapped out the words, but Penelope noted that he had not balled a fist, nor stood up in anger. This meant he was either not very angry at all, or that he was controlling his absolute rage well. Either way, it signalled to her that his actions were being subdued in some way, which unnerved her.

'You seemed insistent that Dr Simmons had his brutal way, Father. She is so delicate in her condition, and bleeding is abhorrent.' Penelope met her father's angry glare.

'Ah! I have a daughter who, it

appears, desires to be in training for clandestine work of subterfuge, but now has the capacity to read thoughts of man and is an authority on matters physical.' He sat back and looked from one to the other of them. 'How could I have been so blind as to not see the genius within my own offspring?'

Penelope now understood this was controlled rage. She shifted uneasily on her seat.

'I assure you our intentions are well-meant; we seek only the well being of Mrs Rose,' Lucas offered his reassurance.

'And you think that I, her husband, do not.' Her father's head tilted slightly as he posed his loaded question.

'I think your actions were swayed by your friendship with Dr Simmons. You see, Mr Lucas Bleakly is also a doctor,' Penelope explained.

'Dr Simmons comes from a long line of eminent physicians,' her father said, then stared at Lucas. 'So you do not follow in the footsteps of your father, but strike out on your own and better him.' Mr Rose stood up and stared into the empty grate of the large fireplace. He rested one hand on the ornately decorated marble mantelpiece. 'So, Dr Bleakly, what have you discerned from your cursory examination?'

'That your wife's heart is weaker than it was, but that her current malaise has been caused by the strength of the opiate she has been subscribed. The heat brought her low, and possibly that — combined with the fashion she wears — may have caused her faints; but if she is continually drugged at such strength, she will not appear sufficiently recovered by Friday, and so further excessive treatment will then appear necessary.' He finished his words carefully.

Her father's fists now balled. 'You did not come to me, Penelope, with any of this.' He glanced at her.

'Father, there was no time. I only found out this morning that Lucas was a doctor.' Penelope saw Esther look up, and she realised she had said too much.

'How so? Did you read his mind also?' her father asked.

'I came to offer my services, sir,' Lucas jumped in, rather more quickly than he needed to.

Whilst still staring at Penelope, Mr Rose replied, 'Thank you for your assistance in this matter, Lucas. I appreciate your well-intended actions, but would ask that you leave and trust my wife's care to my consideration. So there will be no need for you to lurk behind the drapes in my home with my daughter anymore.'

'Sir, there was never any impropriety intended. I behaved badly and I apologise for this.'

Her father spun around as Lucas stood up and smiled broadly at him. 'You have no need to concern yourself. We shall look forward to seeing you at dinner on Friday. Please give my regards to your mother.'

There was no denying the implication. Lucas nodded and gave a courteous gesture to Penelope before leaving.

Esther saw him out, leaving Penelope looking at her father who silently glared back at her.

'Father . . . '

'Daughter, you have embarrassed me. You have disobeyed me. You have wilfully gone against what you believed to have been my intentions, and you have stood alone with a man in full view of the estate. You have coerced your servant into obeying your whims, and you have fraternised with a man alone on the moor road. If I saw you, then others could have. You have disgraced yourself and disappointed me.' He took a long silent breath in.

'Father, I . . . '

'You will go to your room. You will be taken there by Cuthbertson and she will lock you in. A tray will be brought with food for you throughout the rest of this day. It will be plain, little and simple. You will think upon your actions and the implications that could have been spun from them. You will also think on how you betrayed your father's trust. I will speak to you in the morning, when I have calmed; but for now, Penelope, remove yourself from my vision!'

He stared back at the empty grate.

Penelope's hands were trembling, her heart breaking at causing so much distress in only a few hours of the day. She felt so sorry for Lucas, for the embarrassment caused to him; and for her mother, who she wanted to help.

'May I sit with Mama?' she asked in a timid quiet voice.

'No!' He looked down at her, and for the first time in her life she actually shrank back under the rage she saw in his eyes. 'Cuthbertson!'

Esther appeared in the doorway. 'Yes, sir?'

'Escort Miss Penelope straight to her room. Lock the door and return the key to me. You may retrieve it at the hours of one, four and seven, when she may have a small bowl of broth and a slice of bread.'

'Yes, sir,' Esther said, and stepped outside as Penelope walked past her and began to climb the stairs in silence. The trembling had subsided slightly as her anger grew. The man was a bully and cared not for her mama's welfare. She would not be outwitted. She slipped her hand into the pocket and found the bottle of medicine. Once inside her room, she quickly closed the door.

'I'm sorry, miss, but at least this way you can't get into any more trouble, can you?' Esther smiled at her as if to lift her spirits.

'I need your help,' Penelope said, and watched the other woman shake her head.

'You never learn. What will it take, your father beating you? Honestly, miss, I should not test his temper more.'

'I need you to replace this on Mama's side table before this evening.' Penelope held the bottle up. Esther went to take hold of it, but Penelope withdrew it.

'First there is something I must do.' She proceeded to pour a little out of the window. Happy she had reduced it by two-thirds, she then refilled it to the liquid's previous level from her jug of water. 'There, now it is the correct strength.' Penelope gave it a shake and then held it out for Esther to take.

The woman did, but was not happy. 'I hope God in heaven is watching on, because if this is wrong, miss, then . . .'

'It is not. I have complete faith in Lucas's judgement.' Her declaration was bold, even surprising herself.

'Aye, you do. But you judge your father harshly, miss, and that is what has cut him deeply. I will be back at one o'clock with your broth.' She locked the door behind her and Penelope was left in an empty room, feeling more hurt by her father's actions than wounded by his words.

14

The day was long, but Penelope heard no more from her father, and Esther had been given strict instructions not to stay and talk with her. She was only informed that her confinement had been extended to give her more time to think.

Two days passed by before the door was finally unlocked. It was Friday; and the dinner party, as far as she knew, was still to be held.

Penelope nearly burst out of the door, thinking it would be Esther standing in her way, but she was instead surprised and delighted to see her mama standing there in front of her.

'You are well!' Penelope rushed forward and hugged her.

'Be still, child.' Her mother patted her on the back of her shoulders. 'What a mess you make of things — when I am not here to guide your hand, that is.'

'Oh, I . . . ' Penelope hardly knew what to say, for how could she when her mother might not know quite what a mess she had managed to make? It was not her first one, but it was the worst.

'You look well, Mama,' she said, genuinely meaning her words.

'And you, my girl, do not.' Her mother took hold of Penelope's hand. 'You will join me at breakfast. You will then be able to tell me why I find you locked away here by your doting father.'

Penelope bit her lip.

'Oh, do not think of withholding anything from me. I can see plainly how far Father's little star has fallen from the sky — or is at least cowering behind a very dark cloud — in his estimation at the moment.' She laughed. 'Perhaps I should take my rest more often. It seems that you actually care greatly for me, which is indeed comforting to know.'

'Mama, of course I do!' Penelope said, her eyes moistening.

'Then it would not hurt you to show it more often, would it?' Her mother led her like a child out onto the landing and down the stairs. Penelope felt so relieved to be free again, but her emotions were confused. She had not realised just how detached from this woman she had become. How so? She simply wanted different things in life, and resented being formed into the perfect homemaker. She did not want to play piano or sing to a group of guests; she wanted to ride, and walk, and travel. Was that so wrong? Penelope knew these were not considered the correct focus of a young woman of marital age, and felt guilty. The Hall her mother and father loved so much had become like a prison to her, and her mother had taken on the image of her gaoler. However, having spent days locked in her room on meagre rations, she certainly realised just how much freedom and food she was used to.

They took their seats facing each other across the dining table, and waited until their plates were served to them by Sally.

'You may go, girl,' her mama ordered, so that mother and daughter were left staring at each other.

'Thank you, Penelope.' Her mother picked up her spoon and began to eat her porridge. 'I asked for something plain and filling and this is perfect.'

Her mother's words of gratitude surprised Penelope. At first she thought that it might be sarcasm, but there was no edge to her voice.

'I know what you did for me, and I know why.'

'You do?' Penelope asked, wondering just how much her mother did know.

'Yes, does that surprise you so much? My thanks I give to you because you may have saved me from a far worse fate than exhaustion — thank goodness the heat has abated. I prefer the cold air — it freshens the lungs,' her mother said, and swallowed.

'I acted out of instinct and . . . '

'Love!' Her mother smiled. 'You

acted out of instinct, yes, but that was driven by love. I knew Simmons was an overpaid buffoon, yet I did not realise he was also a charlatan. So the younger Mr Bleakly is owed my gratitude also.' Now her smile broadened into a grin.

'You know he was responsible for the medicine being weakened?' Penelope asked as she felt her cheeks burn.

'Oh he was responsible for far more than that. At first I thought I heard the voices in my sleep. Then I realised they were familiar, and real, and in my bedchamber. I did not want to make a fuss, as I also had heard and understood what was being discussed. I had not taken the poison prescribed by Simmons the night before, you see; I never trusted him or his potions, so spat it out into my chamberpot. Not ladylike, I know.' She chuckled, and then continued, 'He is a sadist. Don't look at me so shocked. If you do not know the word — as I suppose you may not — I mean he enjoys seeing women cower. I have no time for him or his ways.'

'Have you told Father?' Penelope asked.

'He has been away a day, so not properly, no. However, I have a dinner party to arrange for tonight, and I would ask you to help me plan for it.'

'Yes, Mama,' Penelope replied, and for once felt enthusiastic about doing so.

'So, you see, the menu is agreed. The seating plan is done, and that only leaves a trip to town to see if we need anything new to adorn our pretty faces.'

She laughed at her quip, and Penelope thought how the natural colour had returned to her cheeks, which gave her a healthy glow.

'Mama, I am sorry for being a poor daughter.' Penelope blurted the words out, feeling she had been a truly negligent and bad daughter. She had been pampered by her father, spoilt by his attention and gifts and treats, and not realised how dispassionate she had become to her mother's isolation.

'Oh, Penelope! I could not love you more. My heart was breaking, though, and now it is mended and will be strong again — you have mended it.'

Penelope ate her fill and laughed with her mother as they had done when she was younger. It felt good to be alive, and she promised that the next time she saw Lucas on her own, she would show him how she felt. She smiled at the thought, for fate was bringing them close and so she did not doubt that they would be together somehow, some-where — soon, she hoped.

15

Penelope and her mother travelled at a slow speed along the narrow road that cut through their estate to join the main route into Gorebeck. Fortunately, it was not a market day, and despite Penelope's misgivings, her mother was most insistent that they would take the carriage — and their time — and visit the milliner's and haberdasher's before returning to dress for dinner. In the few days Penelope had spent locked away in her bedchamber, her mother had apparently rested, having taken time to reconsider her relationship with her daughter. The daughter had ironically been doing the same. The days were now cooler, and so her mother regained her strength. However, there was more to it than that, because she could plainly see the woman looked more alive and happier than she had done so in months, if not a year or so.

'Tell me, Penelope, why do you stare at me so?' she asked.

'I was just thinking how well you look, Mama. The enforced rest has done you much good.'

'I think you are quite correct,' she replied.

'So tell me, Mama, what is to be done about the butcher Simmons, though? Something should be,' Penelope asked.

'I should admonish you for being so bold. It troubles me that he will sit at our table this evening. But the man has status, family and influence. It is not easy to disclose wrongdoing of such a person. He is held in high regard amongst the older members of society. It is they who have influence. Your young Mr Bleakly . . . ' She paused as Penelope objected.

'He is not mine, Mama!'

'Well, not yet, but if you play your cards well enough, you might just snare yourself a good man in him. He has character, my dear; he reminds me of Willis when he was younger. As I was saying, he is full of education and ideas, but has not built up a reputation and name for himself. In fact, if anything, he has built up a rather bad one because he has defied his father.' She looked out of the window as they crossed the old stone bridge. Penelope saw the spire of the ancient Norman church, which announced that they had entered the main street of Gorebeck.

'How well do you know Mr Willis Bleakly?' Penelope asked, and was surprised when her mother tilted her head on one side and looked at her curiously.

'Why do you ask that? You know well enough how long I have lived here, and that he has been our priest for many of those years.' Her mother looked out of the small window as they neared the shops on the new street.

'I ask how well you know him, Mama, not how long. We are being candid with each other, aren't we?'

Penelope watched as her mother bit her bottom lip and then smiled. Her eyes were almost twinkling with amusement.

'Well, let me see. We threw food at each other once. We climbed haystacks together once. We swam in the river once together . . .'

'You did what!' Penelope snapped the words out as the coach lurched to a stop near the millinery shop. Her mother's face was full of mischief as she had spoken. Penelope had never seen her behaving so frivolous in her manner.

'We swam together once. In the pool that you used to slip off to when you were younger. You see, Willis and I shared a home together when I was young. His father was in the Americas for a time — missionary work, or some such. His mother had gone to London for the Season and Willis stayed at our manor house. He was quite a character back then. Not only daring, but handsome — not as much as your Lucas, but similar. We were but children, and he had to go away to school when he was twelve. It was hard for both of us. I became a young lady and he was moulded by the system into what he should be.' She stopped and looked at Penelope, who was staring in disbelief at what she was hearing.

'Did you think you got that wild streak from your father, child? Oh dear, I have played my part too well, have I not? Willis is my closest friend and always will be. He changed, though. He had a hard time at school, and hated it. It hardened him, he lost his daring. It was as if they had broken that beautiful spirit of his. So when we are together, we are like the children we once were again. Except, of course, we no longer chase each other over haystacks!' She smiled.

'Do you love him still?' Penelope asked coyly.

'Yes — as a dear, dear friend. No more. I think that is enough questioning of my virtue, don't you, Penelope? Now, we must alight and choose our finery, for we need to be back to dress for dinner. We will meet our guests in the drawing room at six and have dinner served by seven. I cannot abide it any later, no matter what they set as a fashion in London.' She leaned forward, ready to leave the carriage.

'Mama, do you still love Father?' Penelope said softly as her mother's head was level with hers.

'Come, Penelope, enough tittle-tattle for now. We both need to look our best this evening and I'll not be rushed. I have only just found my feet again, as it were.' She side-glanced at her daughter and quickly added, 'You go, child, and ask your father if he loves me.' She stepped out. Glancing back, she added, 'If you dare be so bold with him as you have been with me.'

Penelope filled her cheeks with air and blew it out slowly before stepping out onto the pavement. At the beginning of this amazing week, she would have expected her mother to have rebuked her severely for being 'so bold';

yet now, after recent events, she had merely avoided answering that question by deflecting it to her father. Would she dare ask him? A few days earlier, she most certainly would have, as they had shared many a confidence over the years — but now? He wouldn't even look at her, let alone talk to her, since he had seen her with Lucas in her mother's bedchamber. The question in her mind was not whether he loved her mother, but: Did he still love his daughter?

'Ah, Mrs Rose, what a splendid surprise to see you up and about and looking so well.'

The now-familiar voice cut across Penelope's thoughts. She too stepped out into the daylight to see Lucas looking fine in his top hat, single-breasted tailcoat and trousers. He cut a fine figure. Penelope was now pleased that she was wearing her new hat and emerald Spencer.

'A double delight, Miss Rose.' He bowed slightly.

'Lucas, why so formal when you two know each other so well?' her mother asked and Penelope saw his eyebrows raise slightly as he looked at her for clarification, as if she had told all to her mama.

'Mama . . . ' Penelope began.

'You see, Lucas,' her mother whispered and smiled at him, 'whilst you were wrapped in my drapes with my daughter, I was laid abed listening to your correct diagnosis and assumption regarding the medication prescribed. It did not seem timely to say anything then, and I was still dulled by it. However, now I am fine, thanks to you two. So fear not, I shall not say anything when we dine tonight. But do take more care in future.' She looked from one to the other.

'I can only apologise and take full responsibility for what happened,' he said.

'Of course you can, but you should not: my daughter is quite capable of getting herself into corners where trouble is concerned — in a very respectable way, may I add.' She smiled at them both. 'But you have my gratitude and I am your friend. So join us this evening as such.'

'My pleasure.' He bowed slightly again and went on his way. Penelope admired the confident way he walked,: not arrogant, but as if he knew his worth.

'Penelope . . . Penelope . . . '

'Yes, Mama, I was just . . . '

'Yes, I know what you were doing — but not here and now. You really have to put that heart back in place,' she said.

'Pardon?'

'Well, we can't have it displayed so on the sleeve of your new Spencer, can we? Come, we are being watched.'

16

Penelope entered the drawing room a little early so that she would be there to greet their guests as they arrived. Her mother would be down shortly; she was still fussing over her hair adornment.

Penelope's dress was simple in design, but made of a lovely soft silk. The high-waisted sapphire fabric hung straight, showing her slender, elegant frame. The square neckline was edged with scalloped lace. The matching ribbons threaded through her fair hair reflected the beauty of her eyes. The effect was one of understated radiance. Penelope was quite pleased, as she preferred simplicity of line to elaborate trimmings or busy floral patterns.

It was the quiet before the business and noise began, she thought, as she stood by the mantelpiece admiring the way the room had been arranged. It was when she realised her father was sitting in the window seat opposite the fire that her cheeks took on a deeper shade of pink than she would have preferred.

They had not spoken since he had had her imprisoned in her room. She felt the anger rise within her, and she struggled to subdue the defiant thoughts from showing in her eyes.

'Penelope, you look the picture of an innocent, beautiful young maiden.' He stood up and walked over to her.

'Thank you, Papa,' she said in as soft a voice as she could muster. She smiled at him, but her heart was sad, and it was the most unusual sensation: each assessing the other as if they had somehow betrayed and broken their precious bond.

'It just goes to show how looks can be so deceptive,' he added, his eyes staring down into hers, accusing and unkind.

'I do not know what you mean, Father. We have guests arriving soon. Perhaps, if you wish to discuss this with me at a more opportune moment, then such a time may be found tomorrow once the party is over.' She spoke with confidence that her mind hardly felt.

'And still, Penelope, you speak out. What must I do to subdue that indomitable spirit of yours? Is it not enough that you have shamed yourself before one of our guests and embarrassed me by taking matters into your own hands? Now you seek to stand before me as if you have every right to answer me back.' He stood with his hands behind him, folded over his tailcoat.

'Father, whatever I did, I only did for Mother's well-being, not to be a rebellious daughter . . . and is she not looking fine again?' Her voice was low, for she did not wish the servants who waited outside the room to bring in refreshments to their guests to hear of any discourse between them.

'What you two did by removing the medication prescribed by Dr Simmons is obstruct a private investigation that I was working on. You took the bottle and adulterated it before I could arrange for Dr Marks, a fellow physician — and, as it happens, a magistrate — to look at it and assess its relevance to her illness. So, instead of assisting me in uncovering the ways of a man of bad or evil practices, you destroyed the evidence.'

'But, Mama, she would have, could have, died of the drug . . . '

'Codswallop! She played her part well enough. Good gracious, girl, do you think that I would allow her to be harmed in any way? She slept, and would have slumbered heavily. But she would not have been bled — do you think I would have that man's butcher of an associate cut my own wife? Have you no faith in me or sense in your head?'

Her father's face was flushed. His voice, though, was controlled, which made his rage seem even more dangerous, and yet Penelope could not stop the words from falling from her lips. 'Do you love Mama?'

He looked at her as if she had slapped his face. He stepped back and shook his head as if her words were somehow ringing in his head.

'Ah, there you two are!' Her mother, looking at least ten years younger than her age, entered the room in a sumptuous maroon gown with Belgian lace trimmings. 'Now, how do I look, Sebastian?'

Penelope watched as her father, who had leant with one hand against the marble mantelpiece as if to regain his balance, stood straight. Her mother's skirt billowed out as she elegantly spun around. The diamante tiara on her head glistened from the light of the chandelier above.

'You look divine, my dear. The rest has done you good.' He then turned, stared out of the window, and saw their coach returning. She saw him swallow, but his eyes did not seek hers; and, as their emotions were obviously running high, neither sought to heighten them further.

'That will be the Bleaklys. I sent the coach to fetch them as I did not want Lucas to have to walk. I doubt Willis would make it up the drive if he had to do so.'

'Sebastian!' her mother rebuked, but her father smiled genially.

'Just teasing, my sweet,' he explained, and walked to the door. 'I will greet our guests whilst you ladies light up the room.'

Her mother looked at her accusingly. 'What have you said to him?' she asked.

'Nothing, Mama . . . that is, nothing you would not have me say.' Penelope smiled as Mrs Bleakly entered, complete with her feathered velvet turban and matching puff-sleeved dress in deep burgundy. She was somewhat shorter than Penelope and her mother, so the empire line made her look quite stocky, but Penelope thought that the striking yellow long-sleeve gloves provided an interesting distraction.

'My dear Mrs Rose, how marvellously well you look,' the woman gushed. She then pinched Penelope's cheek. 'And you, my dear, are the picture of elegant health.'

Penelope saw Lucas grin at this gesture.

'Thank you, Mrs Bleakly; you look quite striking yourself,' she said, and fixed a grin on her face as the woman fanned herself in an act of humility.

Penelope thought this was going to be a very long evening as she saw her father and Willis Bleakly give each other a cursory nod, but then her eyes met Lucas's and an impish smile played on his lips. Then again, perhaps not, she thought, as she joined in the polite chatter that was expected before dinner. Once they were seated at the table, the conversation would flow more freely, as would her father's best wine.

17

Penelope was seated between Mr Bleakly and her father, who took his rightful place at the head of the table. Mrs Bleakly sat to his left, and Penelope to his right. Lucas was shown to the chair next to his mother, directly opposite where Dr Simmons had positioned himself. Her mother, Penelope thought, looked quite genteel as she took her chair facing her husband.

The food was served up promptly: the roast hare, with its head positioned erect, seemed to be staring blankly and directly at Penelope. She had never found heads on the dishes attractive, no matter how skilfully they had been placed — they just looked sad to her, which she found always affected her appetite to eat them. Other courses were placed on the table and politely passed around from one guest to the other.

The wine was poured, drunk with relish by the men, and glasses were refilled in a smooth, almost unnoticeable, fashion. They had one footman attending, who also served their father as a valet and butler. Jarvis was a very busy man, but Sally helped out on such occasions. Esther was ferrying the food from the kitchen to the sideboard in the dining room, taking away empty plates as they were cleared.

Penelope let most of the men's conversation drift over her as she, for once, took note of the comings, goings and silent glances that the servants exchanged; the silent witnesses to her family's life in the Hall, her home. The talk was becoming more animated, though, as the men's voices grew louder.

'I tell you, the humours have explained much for centuries, and we should not delve into the realm of playing God by dissection and all manner of abhorrent experiments,' Dr

Simmons explained.

Under the scrutiny of her father, Penelope had deliberately avoided staring at Lucas, although she had noticed how he had the long fingers that would make an excellent pianist. However, they looked as though they were more used to holding the reins of a horse rather than tinkling the delicate keys of ivory on a grand piano. His voice, sounding a little firmer or vexed, caught her attention.

'Surely the more we know about the inner workings of the body, and how the parts operate together, the broader our knowledge will be; and so we can develop new ways to treat common ailments that are less barbarous than those that have been around for decades, if not centuries.' Lucas was staring at Dr Simmons, the challenge in his words almost tangible.

'Lucas,' his father said, 'mankind should not try to do the work of God. Dr Simmons is quite correct. Goodness, what with body-snatchers . . .

pardon my mentioning such evildoers, ladies.' He turned to his wife and Mrs Rose briefly.

'Precisely, Reverend!' Dr Simmons agreed. 'I come from a line of learned men who swore by the very four humours: blood, choler, phlegm and melancholy! If the basic juices of our being change their rhythm within our skins, then our behaviour is affected and we become ill. Letting out excess can restore our natural vitality. If something is not broken, you do not need to fix it.' He picked up his fork again and was about to place a piece of pork in his mouth when Lucas spoke out.

'Then it would be folly to treat someone who appears to be deep in melancholia with bleeding. Many die in disease because we do not know enough to 'fix' them. The old thinking needs challenging, and an enlightened, open-minded generation needs to take the world of medicine forward by dispelling with myths and superstition and dealing with the science.' He was staring directly at Simmons, who dropped his fork to his plate.

'Dr Simmons, your glass is nearly empty. Sally, do not fall asleep, girl.' Penelope's mother interrupted to cause a distraction, which might have worked had Lucas not continued.

'The French are developing a healthier approach to the science of pathology and making new discoveries. They are . . . '

'Barbaric!' Reverend Bleakly broke in. 'We should all know this by now, having been embroiled in a long war with their 'Emperor'.' He was staring at his son, Penelope thought in a silent plea for him to back down.

'Father, I really meant that . . . '

'I think, gentlemen, we bore the ladies. Talks of such matters are tedious to the more refined amongst us. Perhaps our conversation could continue whilst they retire to the drawing room and we enjoy our port.' Sebastian looked to his wife to take over.

'Excellent notion.' Mrs Rose stood up, and Mrs Bleakly and Penelope followed.

* * *

Penelope managed to give Lucas a quick, appreciative smile as she left; his eyes seemed to acknowledge it, but his manner was still set for the discussion.

Once the ladies had departed, Penelope's father raised a glass. 'Let us toast to our good fortune; that, despite the war, we and our families are here to enjoy the good food of my estate.'

The glasses were raised in silence as they drank. It was only when there was a crash at the end of the room that the momentary peace was broken.

'Quickly, woman, fetch the broom!' Jarvis the footman-cum-butler ordered Esther, as she had dropped a glass.

Esther ran out of the room. She was so upset that she had to pause momentarily outside the door to calm her breathing and gather her emotions as tears welled up. They could drink their fill in self-satisfaction that their families were whole, but she had nothing and no one. And the reason for this — the man who had caused her Henry's death — was sitting in the room. How she wished that the toast would choke him. Reverend Bleakly . . . how tempting it would be to just take the carving knife and end his worthless life, then join her Henry as a consequence. But her Henry would be in heaven, and she cursed to hell, so she would not be able to. She was about to move off when she heard the voices

'Wasn't that Cuthbertson's widow?' Reverend Bleakly asked.

'Yes,' replied Mr Rose. 'She would have starved or been forced to take the parish charity in the poorhouse, so I gave her work here. She is a good sort, just perhaps misguided in marriage. Henry had the tendency to speak his mind openly.'

Esther was pleased that she was

thought highly of by the master of the house, but her pride prickled at his reference to her Henry.

'Many in the area were involved with smuggling . . . ' Lucas began saying.

'Yes, but not Cuthbertson,' his father explained.

That confused Esther — why would he explain that, when he had been the one who had framed him?

'Dr Simmons, you are very quiet on the subject,' Lucas said.

'What is there to say? Many have bought the goods that kept our tables and cellars well-stocked from the free traders. Napoleon may have tried a blockade and other methods to under-mine our way of life, but ingenuity always finds a way. Cuthbertson tried to step above those around him, as if he were better than them, and in so doing he set himself apart. The natural order will always keep its balance: if you let the bad blood out, the balance is restored.'

'Well, if that is so, the man paid for

his beliefs dearly.' Lucas's response sounded vexed.

'Indeed, as we all must,' his father agreed.

'Come, gentlemen, I believe I can hear Penelope playing a fine tune. Let us break with formality and take our port through.'

Esther ran off to get the broom, wiping her tears away, realising she had almost cursed — and would have murdered — the wrong man. Yes, Reverend Bleakly may have looked the other way when the goods were landed and stashed — but Dr Simmons was the one that liked letting out blood; and, as sure as hell existed, Esther knew it was he who had let her Henry's seep away.

18

Penelope played the pianoforte and Lucas turned the pages of the music for her. Her mother, Mrs and Reverend Bleakly, and Dr Simmons made up a four at cards, whilst her father observed them.

This gave Penelope and Lucas precious moments together.

'Are you well?' he whispered into her ear.

She liked the feel of his warm breath as it drifted across her skin.

'Yes, but Papa is still angry . . . ' she said, pausing as she focused on a particularly challenging section. 'He had sought to trap Dr Simmons, using the medication prescribed as proof,' she added quietly.

'And I had you destroy the evidence,' he said, and sighed. 'I am so sorry,' he added. 'How were we to know?'

'I should not have doubted him so,' Penelope replied; but as she glanced up saw, once the players were engrossed in their own gambling world, her father stride casually over to Lucas and her as she played.

Penelope tried to focus as well as she could and not lose the tempo, rhythm, or her place as Lucas diligently leaned in to turn the music once more. She liked his closeness, his musk, the deft skill with which he did things; and, at dinner, his ability to stand his ground for what he believed in. However, her father's presence coming so near to them did not make her feel anything but a cool, detached distance between her and her own kin.

'Your daughter is gifted, sir,' Lucas said, as he continued to follow the notes she played.

'Indeed, she has the gift to meddle in affairs that do not concern her and to create problems for her elders as a result. However, Lucas, I gather you too are equally matched in this aspect of life.' He casually sipped his drink.

Penelope kept playing. She had had a hard teacher who would try to distract her when she played and then rebuke her firmly if the music suffered, so Penelope knew that a good hostess should keep her attention no matter what the guests around her said or did. Besides, with Lucas there, she felt protected. That thought was indeed a strange one, because she had been so close to her father throughout her life, and Lucas was really no more than a new acquaintance — yet fate had drawn them close.

'I think you are being harsh, sir,' Lucas replied. 'Not on me, but Miss Penelope only sought to help. She was not to know you were behaving badly yourself because you had other plans of your own.' He turned a page.

She heard her father laugh. 'Yes, had I met you in town before you became my daughter's white knight, you could possibly have been of some use instead of thwarting what I suspected was to have been the man's undoing. However, patience is a virtue, and another opportunity may well present itself in the future.' He watched his daughter, but she did not take her eyes from the sheets in front of her.

'But how many people will he injure by then, sir?' Lucas said under his breath.

'Perhaps we can speed the process along,' Penelope offered, as she reached the final page of the sonata she was playing. She favoured Haydn, whereas her father preferred the music of Beethoven. However, she was not in the mood to please him; she had been left too long in her room. He had wanted her to think — and indeed she had — of a day when she would have a husband, and no longer be answerable to her father.

'It would be rather obvious, child, if you were to suddenly faint.' Her father looked over to the card players as she played her final notes. They had the good grace to stop and applaud her skills. But she stood quickly before being trapped into playing further pieces.

Penelope smiled, acknowledging their gratitude; and, as soon as they returned their attention to their cards, she looked at her father directly. 'No, I would not be so blatant, but we could enlist the aid of another who would willingly feign illness.' Her voice was low and her emotions controlled.

Her father stared at her and smiled.

'If I may suggest an alternative solution . . . ' Lucas joined in. 'If we visited the Hendersons of Beckton, I believe the father ails and has had the attention of Dr Simmons. I would have visited already; however, it is a little awkward. If Miss Henderson and her dear mama were otherwise engaged with another social engagement, then I might be free to see the man myself — but if they caught me, I would not get past them.' He looked at Penelope, appealing for help. He obviously did not cherish the company of Miss

Henderson, and that pleased her greatly.

'I could arrange a visit, Papa, with my companion and Mama. Then Lucas could arrive with his father to see how Mr Henderson fares.'

There was a squeal of delight as Mrs Bleakly won the final hand. The game had ended, and so the group made its way to the sofas positioned around the ornate fireplace.

'Come, Penelope, let us play charades!' her mother exclaimed, much to Mrs Bleakly's further delight.

Her father nodded at her. 'Go on, Penelope; you should showcase your further gifts, as I know you are a natural for them.'

His words stung because of his meaning, but she turned away from him and was delighted to see that Lucas had followed her to sit near where she stood. He animatedly joined in, and guessed the novel that was miming correctly. Penelope took her seat where he had been, and watched his every gesture with excited eyes until she too guessed his Shakespearean play accurately.

'How well they know each other's minds,' her mother remarked to her father.

'Indeed,' he agreed as he finished his drink in silence, watching and observing two young people falling in love.

19

It was after church on the following Sunday that Penelope next met Lucas. His father had sent him over to her and her mother whilst he bid goodbye to the last of the congregation. Penelope was beginning to see Willis Bleakly in a different light. A spirit crushed by a hard educational system . . . but perhaps some of it still lingered when he was with his childhood friend. She watched Lucas stride over, and could not help but smile at him. He was tall, but not so that she had to crane her neck awkwardly. She rather liked his dark looks: he could appear moody when not smiling, and yet, when he did, his eyes brightened genuinely with the gesture.

'Mrs and Mrs Rose,' Lucas politely greeted her parents, and then looked directly at her. 'Miss Penelope.'

'Your father gives a very direct, if not long, sermon these days, Lucas,' her father responded, and stifled a yawn. Mrs Rose dug him discreetly in the ribs.

'He does indeed, but I am here on a mission of my own, sir. Mrs Rose, my mother bids you would stop by and have tea with her.'

Penelope's mother smiled and looked up at her husband, who nodded. 'That is an excellent idea, we will.' She watched as Lucas shifted his balance.

'I was wondering if I may borrow your husband and daughter for a few moments.' He looked at Mrs Rose with the utmost sincerity, and with what Penelope could only describe as 'puppy-dog eyes'.

'Of course, yes. Where is Cuthbertson? She can accompany me.' Her mother was content to go along with his plan, whatever it was, but Penelope could tell that curiosity was gnawing at her.

Esther Cuthbertson was standing a

few feet behind them. Penelope and Lucas looked anxiously at each other at the prospect of her entering the vicarage, but Penelope's father shook his head slightly to prevent them from uttering a word against it.

Once the two women were set upon the pathway that led to the vicarage's front door, Lucas suggested that they should climb into their carriage. It awaited their return to the Hall and was parked alongside the road nearby.

'Please do tell me what this subterfuge is about, Lucas,' her father asked as he sat on the cushioned seat. Penelope sat opposite him, and was pleased when Lucas chose to position himself by her side, facing her father.

'Dr Simmons is away to Ripon for a few days. He has business there concerning a bet and a race. So now is an excellent time to visit Mr Henderson. Mother has heard that he intends to return with that butcher he calls a surgeon, and has prescribed an elixir to stable the man's melancholia. However, he was not melancholic until he began taking the medicine. His ailment seems to have been a moist cough. It could have been no more than a heavy cold or pneumonia — but I think it is due to one of Simmons' opiates. I have been making enquiries for some months, and have managed to bribe a clerk in York and have copies of orders of two of his basic drugs that he uses — one is a stimulant, and one suppresses the spirit. What interested me was he seems to use the stimulant in higher quantity. Yet, as I have shadowed him these last months, his patients seem to have been subdued — with the exception of one lady who I visited recently.' He stared at her father.

Penelope listened intently, but looked for clarification as she tried to fathom what he meant.

'Opium is a habitual drug that becomes addictive. It sends the senses into a delusional state.' He paused and looked at her father as he seemed to choose his words carefully. 'Some have taken it because initially it has made them feel better about their life, but it is no more than an elixir of the Devil that lures the weak minds into its lair. It can be watered down to laudanum, a commonly used medication. I do not believe Mr Henderson would imbibe such a potion if he knew what it was that he had been given.' Lucas was leaning forward slightly. He had obviously been trying to snare Dr Simmons. He cared for people, wanted to help them and stop them being abused by those who sought financial gain at any cost. How Penelope admired his spirit and sense of justice.

'But what does Dr Simmons gain by this?' she asked.

'Money,' her father said. 'A foot in the door of another wealthy house and a reputation for finding a cure, when in reality he is providing the ailment by making a patient appear worse than they are. I suspect he has given that woman a drug to make her appear irrational, enabling her husband to place her in a lunatic asylum under the falsehood of suffering from hysteria.'

'Whyever would a man do that to his own wife?' Penelope was appalled that such a situation would be true.

Lucas and her father exchanged knowing looks. 'Simply so that the man could claim her entire fortune and enjoy the comforts of his mistress unencumbered by a critical society. For who would deny a man some enjoyment in life when his wife had fallen so low? He spends, buys his friends their desires, and is pitied in turn, whilst his wife languishes in a living hell.' Her father's fists clenched, and she could have sworn that his eyes moistened in the dim light inside the vehicle.

'Can we not help her? You know who she is, and where?' Penelope asked.

'Yes, my dear, I do. For the lady is my cousin, and I intend to prove that the man is a charlatan: that the motive for destroying her sweet character is purely monetary, and that he and his butcher have caused more harm than cure. So we shall call upon the Hendersons this afternoon; and you, your mother, and the inquisitive Esther Cuthbertson shall keep the Henderson women fully absorbed in talk of your own forthcoming engagement, whilst I visit Jeffrey Henderson with my good friend who is a physician and a magistrate. You, Lucas, will stay out of this, for there will be scandal here if you are drawn in . . . and you are just beginning your career.' Her father looked at her. 'And you will not speak out about men's affairs, do you understand me, Penelope?'

'My engagement?' Penelope repeated.

'Yes. I have decided that you two will make an excellent match.' He opened the carriage door and alighted, leaving Lucas and Penelope staring at each other in silence.

20

Penelope took hold of the handle as it fell back into place, closing the door. Lucas's long fingers wrapped around hers, making her hand feel small and protected. She looked up at him as his face was so near to her own.

'Have you nothing to say to your father's bold words? No objections or remonstration?' he asked.

'Have you?' she replied.

Without hesitation he kissed her lips, so tenderly, pulling her to him. She was going to protest; but found, as he removed her hand from the door and placed it by his side, that she leaned into him. The urgency with which she returned his kiss, his touch, his embrace, surprised them both.

The horse moved and the carriage rocked a moment, bringing them back to the realisation that they were canoodling in a private coach outside a church on a Sunday. Penelope sat bolt upright, opened the door, and stepped out. Her father waited by the church wall, his knowing gaze making her quake slightly inside . . . but that was nothing to the surge of feelings that had overtaken her when Lucas had stolen a kiss from her seconds earlier.

'Have you nothing to say, child?' he asked.

Penelope had lots to, but wanted to distract her father as she needed to speak further with Lucas. 'Yes, I do, Father. If Dr Simmons has bought a quantity of drugs that stimulate, then is it possible they would have the same effect on animals — such as a horse?'

Her father looked completely taken aback. Lucas looked at her and laughed. Then the two men stared at each other.

'It takes a woman to state the obvious, Mr Rose.' Lucas looked at her and smiled. 'His business at the races, his ongoing wealth . . . he is not a gambler, he makes his money on sureties. His patients he can mend — the races he can fix. The man is a complete blackguard.'

Her father shook his head. 'Come with me, Lucas. We need to see my friend Dr Marks urgently. Penelope, you join your mama, then this afternoon the three of you visit the Hendersons. Try and get hold of his medicine, swap the watered-down one you left with your mother in its place. The bottles will be uniform. I am sure that Esther can find a way to slip upstairs to do this. She has no reason to want to protect Simmons. He let her Henry die. We'll need to take Dr Marks with us to Ripon. Return to us at the Hall.'

'Yes, Father,' she said, and he began to walk away. 'Father!' He stopped and glanced back at her. 'Have you nothing else to say?' She swallowed.

'Yes, along with your mother's ability to get into situations, you seem to have inherited a modicum of your father's intelligence.' He walked off.

'Lucas, do you think he will ever forgive me?' she asked.

Lucas patted her shoulder quickly and whispered, 'I think he has, but he is determined that you do not take such risks again. Did he not tell you that he saw you swim?'

'No!' Penelope gasped.

'Yes, dear Penelope. He is determined that we will be wed.' Lucas, who was standing a pace from her, then smiled. 'I must go.'

'But, Lucas, do you . . . I mean, are you . . . ?'

'Yes.' He touched the brim of his tall hat as he stepped away from her to join her father. 'Now, go and join your mother, and remember the tasks we are about. Good day, Miss Penelope.'

Penelope walked briskly to the vicarage. Her cheeks burned. Her heart was filled with such emotions that it pumped ever quicker. The joy of Lucas's touch and the sensations that overwhelmed her whenever they were together . . . and then the sweeping, all-consuming shame that her father had seen her swim — stand near-naked in front of Lucas. She shook her head, looked to the sky. She had wanted to be as a child again, one who played in a pool to get away from the heat and the restrictions of a woman's overwhelming garments. Yet it had been her passage to womanhood for, at that moment, her father had decided she had sealed her own fate. She would marry the man who had looked upon her in such a dishevelled and wanton state. Her eyes shut momentarily.

She knocked on the vicarage door and smiled. She had a part to play, and a future to look forward to. Life would never be dull again.

21

'Three hours we have been here,' Dr Marks said to Penelope's father.

'Yes, I know, sir. But the assizes begins next week, as you are well aware. That means races will be part of the fun after the trials and hangings have been executed. He must be here somewhere. If we find out which horse he has an interest in, then perhaps by association we can deliver on my theory.' Her father was sitting on the settle in the best inn in town. From his vantage point he could see through the window to the street and watch who came and went. But Simmons had not appeared.

'You are certain, Sebastian, of this wrongdoing? His father knew mine. He was a good and talented man, as was his own father. I admit I have been made a little uneasy by some of the things he has said in my presence — he hankers for the old ways — but to fall so low . . . It is beyond inadequacy of skill: it shows a lack of character, it is a crime, and is punishable — severely so.' Dr Marks drank from his tankard and shook his head. 'It is a bad business.'

'There is a worse one. Whilst we wait, I would ask a further favour of your time — for you to visit an unsavoury place with me.' Sebastian was moving his tankard around in his fingers as he spoke.

The magistrate raised an eyebrow. 'What is it, Sebastian? Something burns inside you — what is it?'

'The asylum: he has someone dear to me imprisoned there, unjustly,' Sebastian explained.

'Whatever for?' he asked, his face quite shocked. 'I will see all manner of humanity stand before me next week as I pass sentence. Why would I wish to look at the dregs? Do you have proof of this new accusation of wrongdoing?'

'If you go, you will see for yourself.' Sebastian's desperation showed in his voice and manner as he leaned over the table. 'Because, sir, my cousin has been wrongly diagnosed and incarcerated by Simmons at the will of her husband. I fear for her. She is like a trapped innocent. God, I feel sick when I think of what that beautiful woman may have endured.'

Sebastian swallowed and stared at the man. 'I believe he may have used a similar drug on her to make her appear hysterical, when in fact she was a timid, kindly soul.'

'Is this some kind of vendetta you have involved me in because you do not like the diagnosis against this woman? They are well-known for imbalances — menstrual derangement, and so forth. Is this the real reason I am here — because of this?' His tone changed.

'No, sir, it is not. I would have come direct with that assertion, but I had no proof. Now we gather it. The pointers are all there. William, I do need you to do this. Please?' The man's voice nearly cracked.

'My, my, Sebastian, you let your shell open a little. I can actually see a heart beating inside that cool, calm persona you normally show the world.' He sighed deeply. 'Well, if your horse theory is to bear no fruit, I will use my authority to visit this apparently wronged creature. But, Sebastian, my judgement will not be swayed by sentiment. So she may be left in her 'hell', as you put it, if her state of mind requires it.' He pressed his finger down onto the table to stress his point.

'That is all I ask, William. Use your physician's eye and learning for the good they were intended for, and not for profit, like Simmons has.' Sebastian clenched his lips tightly together.

Dr Marks laughed. 'Man, you have the tact of a wild boar. It is I who gives out judgement and advice.' He shook his head as if few dared speak to him so.

'Yes, sir, of course. Forgive me, I forget myself.' Sebastian smiled, but the muscle in his cheek twitched. He was not used to having to be so humble, but needs must when the Devil drives . . . for he *was* chasing down a devil.

They were joined suddenly by a rushed Lucas. He sat next to Dr Marks quickly, as if he had flown in on the wind. His face animated, it was obvious he was in need to share something urgent with them.

'I thought I told you to stay away!' Sebastian Rose snapped.

'Yes, but while you sup and watch, I find.' He nodded to the magistrate and added, 'Sir, I have found where Simmons is holed up. He is at Bradwell House outside of town. It was when you mentioned your cousin, Mr Rose, I thought I would find out more.' He could not help but grin.

'You cannot keep that nose of yours out of my affairs or family, can you, man?' Sebastian snapped, but Dr Marks was enthralled.

'Continue,' he said.

'Well, Bradwell House is now building a stock of horses based on the success of the last season's races amongst the gentry. His nags won heats against the odds. Of course, as you know, Mr Rose, Bradwell House is the home of your cousin . . . or was.' Lucas stopped and stared at one and then the other of the two gentlemen as the anger showed visibly upon their faces.

'Get the constable, Lucas, and have him bring four armed and trusted men on horseback. They had better be quick. We will go directly to Bradwell House. They will hardly expect such a visit on a Sunday afternoon, but receive us they will!' Dr Marks slapped his hand down on the table, making the ale spill. 'No time for that now,' he said as he pointed to it. 'We must act!'

Lucas set about his given task as the other two gentlemen collected their own horses from the stable lad.

'Come, let us hunt, Sebastian!' Dr Marks said as they set off.

★　★　★

Within thirty minutes they had ridden at speed to the grounds of the Bradwell House. The men went straight to the stables. One man with a blackthorn club had been left on guard. He was outnumbered and outsmarted, and soon had to stand aside.

Dr Marks stormed in. Two horses seemed quite calm, but there was one in the end stall that seemed very skittish. He had the constable's men restrain it, which took some doing, whilst he gave it a quick examination.

'Very well, step back, men.' He turned to Sebastian nodding. 'This animal has definitely been given something to make its eyes wild and its nature erratic. I could guess at what, but why don't we search the stables and see if we can find that actual substance? Fan out, men. We will go to the house and see if we can find Dr Simmons in there with his co-conspirator. This man is arrogant and sloppy; he makes mistakes and is complacent . . . '

'Here, sir.' One of the men rushed up

with a black leather bag that had been left on a stool in an empty stable.

Dr Marks inspected it. 'Damn the man!' He looked to Sebastian. 'We will have them locked up. I feel pity for his poor wife. Let us go to her as soon as these two are arrested.'

Sebastian looked unmoved at the thought. 'Perhaps, if we ask them to accompany us to the asylum, you might find a room there to hold them in until they can be taken to the lock-up and brought before a judge at next week's assizes . . . ' His voice betrayed the cold edge of intent.

'No, Sebastian. We do this correctly. I will go to the house with these men. They will be arrested and taken to gaol. You await me at the gate, and I will ride with you to the asylum. I will not stand by and see you take the law, which I have spent my life upholding, into your own hands.'

Sebastian had no choice but to agree, no matter how desperately he wanted justice done — but he would like to have meted it out himself.

* * *

The Hendersons were most surprised to see Penelope and Esther, but welcomed their guests openly. They entered the drawing room, where tea-making equipment had been laid out on a table for them to share and enjoy the experience. It was also to show off their new set.

Half way through their chatter, Penelope turned to Esther. 'I seem to have lost a glove. Go and see if it is in the coach, please.' Her mother looked at her a little suspiciously, as Penelope had not informed her of what Esther was to do: that way, Penelope thought, she would act innocently — as she was. It seemed to her to be the most convincing way to carry the subterfuge off. 'Take your time; I know you get out of breath when you rush. Most unseemly!'

'Yes, Miss Penelope,' Esther said, as

she discreetly left the room. Mrs Henderson watched her curiously.

'Isn't that woman the . . . ' she began.

'Slow, I know — in wit as well as in gait — but she does well enough,' Penelope's mother said.

'Mama, should we share my news now? After all, we do not want any gossip from the servants, do we? I know it has not been made official yet, but I cannot keep it in anymore. Please?' Penelope asked her mother. She could see the surprise in her eyes, but her face stayed animated, as if she knew exactly what was going to be shared with their hosts.

'Whyever not? Should I perhaps disclose your news . . . or, no — it is *your* news. Please go ahead.' She smiled broadly at her daughter, as if she was enjoying playing this game of tell, but had made Penelope's heart skip a beat when she had offered to take over.

'Well, it is just so exciting! You see, my engagement to Mr Lucas Bleakly is to be announced shortly by my father.' Penelope's eyes almost twinkled with genuine delight, for she was truly happy at the thought. Her mother's small exhalation of breath was not heard because Miss Henderson, who had been sipping her tea, nearly coughed it back out. Penelope knew she would be disappointed, but had not meant to choke her. She was a young woman who had been given everything she asked for in life — but Lucas was not hers to have.

Miss Henderson regained control and smiled falsely, and her mama put on an equally controlled smile that did not reflect in her eyes. They remained sharp and direct as she said, 'Oh, what news. Congratulations, my dear. You will have married into a good family, and I am sure that the stories about his wild days will be placed behind him. You will be such a sobering influence upon him, I am sure.' Miss Henderson nodded.

'Thank you,' Penelope said, but did

not add what she was thinking: which was that she hoped she would not be *too* sobering an influence upon him . . . However, her mother squeezed her hand momentarily. 'It is indeed excellent news.'

'Got it!' Esther's bright voice broke the moment as she re-entered the room, waving the missing glove in her hand. Penelope had to stifle a giggle, as she knew that meant she had swapped the bottles, and had the evidence they were sent to retrieve. However, her companion would be livid that she had missed the best piece of gossip the women had shared all afternoon.

22

The two men entered the austere stone building of the asylum. It was situated in grounds far away from the town. The woman who let them in had a simple grey dress and apron as her uniform. Her hair was roughly tied up and looked like it could do with a good wash. Sebastian braced himself as he saw the bunch of keys hanging from her skirt. They made her appear like a gaoler.

'We are here to see Mrs Charlotte Bradwell Kemp,' Dr Mark explained.

'Does Dr Simmons knows you are here? He's the only one who sees her, like,' she said, and Sebastian felt his stomach clench at the thought of what the man might have done to her.

'How often does he see her?' Dr Marks asked.

'Every last Friday of the month,

without fail,' she said, and as the doctor looked more interested and raised an eyebrow, she looked around her. The noise within the building was bad enough, Sebastian thought, that he doubted anyone would hear anything she was saying.

'She gets so upset when he leaves her. She gets all agitated again and we have to cold-bath her to calm her down. Still, she's settled now, for it is a while since she has seen him. But you can't see her without his permission. Them's the rules,' she said, and gestured to the door as if they would then leave.

'Well, I represent the law, so unless you want to be locked the other side of a door like one of these as someone who tried to prevent a magistrate from upholding it, I strongly suggest that you give me the key to it and show me to her!' His words were snapped out.

'Agnes, you got trouble?' a voice shouted down a stone staircase. It came from a man who looked like the roughest of farm labourers Sebastian had ever seen.

'Um, no, 'tis alright, Brian. You go about setting the baths. I'll be there in a moment.'

'Tell me,' Sebastian asked, his voice almost cracking with rage, 'does that man bathe the prisoners . . . patients?' He took in a deep breath to brace himself for her answer.

'No! Only if they create a fuss; and after the first time, even the most stupid one doesn't make that big a fuss. Well, not the women, anyways.' She sniffed and walked down a corridor that was as grim as he felt. He shut his ears to wailing, shouting, and the clanging of what he presumed were restraints.

The door at the end was opened; and there, despite his worst fears, his beautiful, gaunt-looking cousin was sitting in a chair unpicking some wool. The room had a small bed at one side with what looked like decent sheets and cover. A small rug lay on the stone ground. There was a tiny window high up, where she could see the sky, and that shone light onto the place where her chair was positioned.

She stood up, dropped the wool, and focused on the strange man who entered first. Sebastian saw her hand tremble.

He could not stand it anymore. 'Charlotte!' He rushed forward and embraced her.

She seemed stunned into silence. Then her arms slowly rose and held Sebastian tightly to her.

'Is it really you?' she asked

'Yes, my love, it is.'

'Am I free of this place?' she sobbed.

Sebastian looked at Dr Marks, his eyes moist: pleading for his friend to give the authority to release her — his cousin — the only woman he had ever truly loved, but had been forbidden to marry by his father and hers.

'Yes, you are free of this place, but we will need to make sure that you are fit of mind.'

'I am until I have to take that

medicine. Then I am restrained until he goes . . . '

Sebastian patted her head. 'It is over; he has been arrested.'

Penelope had asked him if he loved his wife. Yes, of course he did — they had been friends for years — though how to define which sort of love it was? But as he held this wronged woman, felt the power of their forbidden love in his arms, he knew which was stronger. He stepped back. He would have her restored to health and what was truly hers, but their love had been forbidden; and instead, he had a kind wife and a beautiful, headstrong daughter. Charlotte would have a new companion in Esther Cuthbertson; he would stand next to her as they saw Simmons hanged for his sins. She was a soul who needed a mistress, and her soon-to-be mistress equally needed her. Penelope and Lucas would have each other; and he, his loyal wife.

He wrapped the blanket around

Charlotte's shoulders. 'Come, we leave now.'

* * *

Lucas rode back late, but Penelope had waited for him. Her mother had gone up to bed and Esther slept in the chair by the fire.

'All is sorted.' Lucas filled her in on the day's events, and also about the reappearance of her father's cousin.

'That is a truly horrid story.' She looked at him.

'Your father will return once he has sorted Charlotte's needs out. So, you see, the area now needs a good doctor, as it is one bad one short!' He smiled.

'Can you settle to it?' she asked.

'It is what I have trained for. Can you settle for the life of a wife of one?' he asked, and brushed a wayward curl of her hair behind her ear, but paused to cup the soft skin of her cheek in his palm. She leaned into the warmth of his skin and kissed it.

'If I may help you sometimes,' she whispered.

'Sometimes . . . '

'If I may read your books sometimes . . . ' she added.

'Sometimes . . . '

'If I can share your little adventures . . . '

He kissed her tenderly. 'Yes, Penelope, always . . . '

MOLLY'S SECRET
CHLOE'S FRIEND
A PHOENIX RISES
ABIGAIL MOOR:
THE DARKEST DAWN
DISCOVERING ELLIE
TRUTH, LOVE AND LIES
SOPHIE'S DREAM
TERESA'S TREASURE
ROSES ARE DEAD
AUGUSTA'S CHARM
A STOLEN HEART
REGAN'S FALL
LAURA'S LEGACY
PARTHENA'S PROMISE
THE HUSBAND AND HEIR